TEAM RACER

BOOKS BY W. E. BUTTERWORTH

AIR EVAC
CRAZY TO RACE
FAST AND SMART
FAST GREEN CAR
GRAND PRIX DRIVER
HELICOPTER PILOT
MARTY AND THE MICRO-MIDGETS
REDLINE 7100
ROAD RACER
SOLDIERS ON HORSEBACK
STOCK CAR RACER
THE WHEEL OF A FAST CAR
RETURN TO RACING
THE HIGH WIND
TEAM RACER

TEAM RACER

W. E. BUTTERWORTH

A W. W. NORTON BOOK

Published by
GROSSET & DUNLAP, INC.
A National General Company
New York

# CHAPTER ONE

STEVE HAAS, DRESSED in a knit sports shirt, a nylon zipper jacket, white Levis and loafers, opened the door of a new, but already battered, Amalgamated Motors Corporation Roustabout, and got out in front of the entrance to Dallas, Texas' Love Field.

The Roustabout, although he wasn't exactly wild about the name, was, Steve thought, one of the better Amalgamated Motors products. If the term "station wagon" had not been reserved for far more elegant, if less practical, Amalgamated models, it would suit the Roustabout. It was all metal, built on the half-ton pick-up chassis, sturdy, practical and comfortable. It was even air-conditioned, something he appreciated immediately when he stepped out of it into the hot Texas day.

He opened the rear door, and took out two pieces

of luggage. Both were of molded fiberglass and both showed signs of a good deal of use. One was a suitcase, the size known as "overnight," and the other was a briefcase, a title not used by the manufacturer, but clung to doggedly by Steve Haas, to whom the words "attaché case" called forth a mental picture of an English diplomat in a derby and striped pants.

"Thanks, Jimmy," he said to the Roustabout's driver, another young man dressed much the same way as Steve Haas. "Appreciate the ride."

"Anytime, Steve," the driver said. He made a little waving motion with his hand, and as soon as the door slammed shut, drove away. The Roustabout carried a strange license plate. It was a Michigan tag with the abbreviation *Mfgr* above the numbers. On each front door, in small black letters, were the words AMALGAMATED MOTORS CORPORATION.

When Steve had gone inside the terminal, walked past the huge statue of the cowboy, and then up the stairs and down a corridor, he found the same words, in the same style of lettering, on a polished oak door. He pushed it open and walked inside.

It was a combination office and waiting room. Amalgamated Motors Corporation, the fourth or fifth largest corporation in the nation, moved so many aircraft in its executive fleet that it was forced to operate very much like an airline. There were similar offices in most of the major airports in the United States and Canada.

Company policy required people traveling on company business to use the company facility wherever there was one. Hopefully, there would be a spare seat on a company airplane also going in the same direction, so the price of an airline ticket could be saved. If there was no flight, the company office would write a ticket on an airline, in very much the same way a passenger would buy a ticket, except that no money changed hands.

There were two people in the room, and although Steve had been here often before, he recognized neither of them, which was a pity, because one of them, the female behind the desk, was the sort of female in which Steve felt a definite interest.

That was more or less reciprocal, too. Steve Haas was a large young man, generally carrying a deep tan along with the 200 pounds on his six-foot frame. He had the large white teeth and the heavy, healthy hair growth of his Moravian ancestors.

"Good afternoon," the young lady behind the desk said with just a shade more enthusiasm than she might have shown a gentleman in his middle forties, and perhaps just a little less enthusiasm than she would have shown if this healthy specimen of a Czechoslovak-American had appeared in a business suit, rather than Levis and a nylon jacket.

"Hello," Steve said. "How's chances of catching a ride to Detroit?"

"May I have your identification card?" the young woman said, and the other man in the room, who could not have helped overhearing the conversation, said:

"You're in luck, buddy. Just as soon as some engineering big shot gets in from the test track, we're off to Detroit. I've got plenty of room."

"Who's the big shot?" Steve asked, as he handed over his company identification card to the young woman with the sort of smile he reserved for young women like this one.

"Haas," the other man, now obviously a company pilot, said, consulting a company flight authorization form. "Stefan V. Haas. Supervisory Engineer, Special Projects. Know him?"

"Captain," the young woman said, "this *is* . . . Mr. Haas."

"That's what's known as putting your foot, shoe and all, in your mouth," the pilot said. "No offense intended, Mr. Haas."

"You're not trying to tell me they sent an airplane down here just to pick me up?" Steve asked, putting his ID back in his wallet.

"Not exactly," the pilot said. "I was down in New Orleans. I was told to stop here and pick you up, instead of going back to Detroit empty."

"Maybe I should ask for a raise," Steve said. "Or maybe they've sent a plane for me so they can fire me quicker."

"Travel authorization's signed by Stuart Whitman," the pilot said. "Vice President, Automotive Engineering."

"He's my boss," Steve said. "I wonder what's up."

"You mean you just happened to be going back to Detroit, anyway?" the pilot asked.

"I got a teletype message this morning, telling me to show up in a suit in Detroit in the morning," Steve said. Then he added with a wry smile, "I don't really think they'd tell me to get dressed up just to fire me, do you?"

"They'd probably have sent you a bus ticket if they were going to fire you," the pilot said. "Anytime you're ready, Mr. Haas, we can leave."

"I wish you'd call me Steve," Steve said, and put out his hand.

"Paul D'Angelo," the pilot said, taking it. "Can I give you a hand with your luggage?"

"Have a nice flight, Mr. Haas," the young woman said. "I hope we'll see you again." Her smile was now unquestionably bright, brighter even than it would have been if Steve had shown up wearing a suit. Like most clever young women in Amalgamated's employ, she hadn't taken long to learn a good deal about the organizational hierarchy. The first fact she had filed away was the code number under Steve's name on the ID card. The company functioned under the notion that first priority for travel should go to those highest in the hierarchy. To identify the relative position of employees in the company, every employee, from the Chairman of the Board to the men who operated the trash trucks, was assigned to a group, with a number. The top echelon brass were assigned a single digit number, from one to nine. Mr. Stuart Whitman, Vice President, Automotive Engineering, of the parent company, for example, was a 4. Managers of assembly plants, district sales managers, and other executives at that level ranged upward to 9. People in the next level of authority were given two digit numbers. Way at the other end of the scale, the trash truck drivers had three digit identification numbers.

Steve's ID code was 22. When she put that fact together with his remark that Mr. Stuart Whitman was his boss, she could easily determine that Mr. Haas, despite the Levis and the zipper jacket, held a position with Amalgamated that was regarded as more important than, for example, that of the pilot of the airplane who was to fly him to Detroit. Most pilots were 55's, with a few 35's, even fewer 20's, those who flew the company jets, and only one Code 9, the chief pilot.

Steve's identity card also gave his marital status, his place of employment, and his home address. The receptionist at the Dallas travel office thought it was a dirty shame that the first bachelor 22 she had ever met, a good-looking one at that, lived in Detroit and might not ever pass through Dallas again.

She had no way of knowing, of course, that as Steve walked with the pilot through the terminal, he commented that he was going to have to plot a way to come through Dallas again.

"They must have made a mistake in Personnel," Steve said. "I thought they had a rule that lady employees had to be 55 years old and grandmothers."

"I just did happen to notice that," the pilot said.

"Well, since we can't take her with us, how about seeing if we can give some GI a ride to Detroit?"

"The airplane's assigned to you," the pilot said. "It's OK with me, if you'll sign the manifest."

"Whitman does it all the time," Steve said. "Whenever he's got a spare seat. I'm sure it would be OK with him."

"You work directly for Whitman?"

"Yeah," Steve said. "I'm sort of an errand boy for the top brass."

That wasn't exactly the truth, the whole truth and nothing but the truth. For one thing, Steve was an engineer. He held a Bachelor of Science degree in automotive engineering, from Michigan State, plus the degree of Diplom Engineur, more or less the German equivalent of an American Master's degree, from the University of Marburg, in Germany. He was carried on the company payroll as a supervisory engineer, a title that reflected how much money he was paid, if it did at the same time give a wrong impression that he supervised other engineers.

Steve and Paul D'Angelo walked through the terminal, looking up at the bulletin boards behind the airlines ticket counters. At one, where there was an announced flight to Detroit, Steve walked to the counter.

"If you've got a GI or two on that Detroit flight, we've got a light plane, and he can ride with us," he said to the ticket clerk.

"I got three," the ticket clerk said, with a smile. "Including one guy who doesn't have a seat and needs a ride." He pointed to three soldiers waiting on the modern plastic and chrome seats, and Steve walked over to them.

"We're going to Detroit in a light airplane," Steve said. "If anybody wants a free ride."

They stood up as if tied together. "Yes, sir," they chorused.

"Let's go," Steve said.

"This is very nice of you, sir," one of the soldiers, a buck sergeant, said.

"Don't call me 'sir,' " Steve said. "I used to wear five stripes myself."

They walked out of the terminal, and over to an Aero Commander, a six-seat, twin-engine airplane sitting, dwarfed, beside a Grumman Gulf Stream. Both aircraft had the AMC logotype on their noses, and the words AMALGAMATED MOTORS CORPORATION painted along their fuselages.

A man in white coveralls came out as the pilot was pre-flighting the airplane.

"Box lunches?" he asked.

"Five, please," Steve said, and in a moment they were delivered.

When he returned with the box lunches, the ground crewman asked, "Who signs for these?"

"He does," the pilot said, nodding toward Steve.

"Can't we pay for these?" one of the GI's asked.

"That would hopelessly foul up the bookkeeping," Steve said. "Next time you buy a car, buy one of ours."

"What do you do for Amalgamated?" the buck sergeant asked. "If you don't mind my asking."

"About the same thing I did when I was in the Army," Steve replied. "I take vehicles apart and put them back together again."

That was closer to the truth than his comment to D'Angelo that he was an errand boy for the top brass.

Stuart Whitman was the chief automotive engineer for the parent company, and as such responsible for the engineering of all the divisions of Amalgamated Motors, all the brand names. When an Amalgamated Motors product was brought into Detroit—or for that matter, a Ford or a Buick or a Chrysler or an Ambassador, for the competition's products were carefully studied—Steve Haas did much of the physical examination, taking them apart to see how they worked and how much a part was worn in service.

He brought to that duty both his knowledge as an engineer and his skill as a mechanic. He'd been a mechanic, and then a motor sergeant in the Army before he went to college, and he thought, as he always did when he was around soldiers, of his Army days now.

He'd come a long way since then. He'd liked the Army, and he'd had the five stripes of a Sergeant First Class on his arm when he was very young. Until he met a reserve officer named Wilson Howell, he had been sure that he would spend his life in the Army, working himself up to Master Sergeant, and then maybe to Warrant Officer. But Howell, who was a college professor in civilian life, had had the strange notion that Steve Haas should go to college himself. Gradually, Howell had worn down what really had been massive resistance to the idea, and finally talked Steve into trying college for 60 days. If he didn't like it, he could go back into the service and keep his stripes.

The first 30 days had been the most miserable of Steve's life, but then, suddenly, some freakish section of his mind had opened, and not only had he been able to compete with the other students, but to excel. He earned his Bachelor's Degree, cum laude, in three years. Then Amalgamated had hired him, because he was a Czech, and spoke German, to go to an

Amalgamated plant in Germany and serve as a sort of translator.

He hadn't actually worked as a translator, but he'd had the chance to go to the University of Marburg, and to work on a special project. It was a racing transmission which was being developed as a joint venture of the German subsidiary, an English racing car manufacturer, and Amalgamated Motors Engineering Division.

When that project was finished, he'd been assigned to work for the Engineering Division. Almost by accident, he'd wound up working for Stuart Whitman himself. While they were making up their minds where to assign him, he had been given first one, and then another, small assignment to take some of the work load off Whitman. Soon that was all he was doing. He filled in for Whitman, did those things Whitman either didn't have the time to do himself, or didn't really want to do.

Steve attended conferences, and took notes for Whitman's benefit. He read the engineering reports which reached Whitman's office by every mailbag and marked with a red pencil those things which he felt Whitman should see. He spent a good deal of time reading technical papers in German, translating those he felt would be of interest to Whitman and other senior engineers.

And odd jobs, too. When the competition's cars came out, and Amalgamated bought one, Steve went and made the purchase. Once, when it had been some brass hat's brilliant idea that Amalgamated should look at the Russian *Zim* limousine, he'd even gone to Vienna and bought one.

He liked his work, and he liked his boss, and he was very much aware that Supervisory Engineer Stefan V. Haas was making a great deal more money than SFC S. V. Haas had ever made.

He'd come to understand that the real beauty of his job was that it was always different. He really never knew from one day to the next what he would be doing the following day. He'd planned to spend at least a week in Texas, watching the testing of a new Fireyear tire on half a dozen cars, doing some of the driving himself, checking wear and ride; yet here he was being ordered immediately back to Detroit after only two days.

He didn't know what was up, but he thought it was probably going to be very interesting, if it was important enough for Whitman to go to the trouble to have a plane routed to take him home.

If luck was with him, it would be a short assignment, one that would be over before the tire testing was over, one that would, in other words, allow him to pass back through Dallas, and just happen to drop in and see the girl in the waiting room at the airport.

When they reached the airport in Detroit, a company car took him home. Steve lived in a hotel. It was an old hotel, far from luxurious, and it had turned many of its suites into apartments for long-term lease. Most of his neighbors were retired people who lived there for much the same reasons he did: It was cheap, and the hotel took care of things they'd rather not take care of themselves, such as cleaning up and making the beds and handling the laundry. The apartment even came equipped with a doll-sized stove and refrigerator.

It had entered Steve's mind, when it had first become apparent that he was going to be around Detroit awhile that what he probably should do would be to buy some furniture, and move into one of the more elegant high-rise apartments, out near the plant.

Price had quickly changed his mind. The only furniture he really liked, when he made a tour of the

furniture stores, seemed to have been designed to
sell to the very rich. When he priced the high-rise
apartments, they seemed intended for the same people who could afford the furniture.

While most of the people who had come to live in
the apartment hotel had added many touches to
make their apartments "homey," there were only
two things in Steve's apartment, other than his clothing and stacks of technical papers of one kind or
another, that had been added to the hotel furnishings. On his dresser was a picture of his mother and
her new husband. She'd married the butcher down
the street shortly after Steve had gone into the Army,
and they seemed to make a happy couple. And hanging in a rack on the wall were a rifle and a shotgun.
Whenever he could find the time, which hadn't been
often, Steve hunted. He had paid his dues, too, and
joined the Amalgamated Engineering Skeet Club,
but he'd only found time to go out to their range
twice.

The D'Arcy Arms Residential Hotel's bellboy was
pushing sixty. Steve could tell by the half-dozen beer
cans in the wastebasket that Ernie had been finding
respite from his labors by hiding out in Steve's apartment. He hadn't seen Ernie as he'd walked through
the lobby, but he hadn't been in the apartment 60
seconds before Ernie came in after him.

"I thought I saw you coming in," he said. "Didn't
like Texas, huh?"

"I hope that's your beer you've been drinking,"
Steve said.

"Of course it is," Ernie replied, in hurt dignity.
And then, remembering: "Some guy delivered this
from the company this afternoon," he said, and
handed Steve an envelope, bearing an Amalgamated
return address.

Steve tore it open:

"My office. 9:00 sharp. And try to look respectable. If you can't make it, let me know tonight. W."

Steve balled the typewritten note up and dropped it in the basket. He debated calling Whitman anyway, even though he could make it, to see what it was all about. But he realized that if Whitman had wanted to tell him what was going on, he would have either telephoned, or explained in the teletype message to Texas, or in this note. He went over his recent activities in his mind, thinking hard, but couldn't think of anything he had done that would have put him in hot water. He shrugged. There was nothing to do but wait and see.

"Ernie," he said, "would I be taking you away from the straight and narrow path of your duties if I offered you a beer?"

"Steve," Ernie said, settling himself in Steve's armchair, "I was afraid you were never going to ask. Tell me all about Texas."

Steve bent and took two cans of beer from his refrigerator and handed one to Ernie. It turned out that what had made the biggest impression on him in his two days in Texas had been the five minutes he'd spent in the company of the girl in the Love Field transportation office.

CHAPTER TWO

AT HALF PAST eight the next morning Steve walked out of the D'Arcy Residential Hotel, and flagged a taxicab. He didn't own a car. Cars, of all sorts, brands, and descriptions were one of the fringe benefits of his job. There were always five or six, and sometimes as many as twenty cars in the fenced-in parking lot behind the Engineering Building on Dearborn Avenue.

Not only was he allowed to use one of them whenever he wanted one, but actually encouraged to. Getting personal experience with the company's cars and those of competition was his business. It was only when he left town for three or four days at a time that he had to worry about transportation.

The Engineering Building of Amalgamated Motors Corporation was a seven-story, ultra-modern

building which looked at first glance to be con-
structed almost entirely of glass. A fountain in front
sent up varying streams of water, and the doors
opened by electric eye as people neared them. Steve
walked to the bank of elevators and rode to the sev-
enth floor. Outside the elevator, a receptionist sat,
discreetly guarding access to the executive offices
beyond an oak door.

"Good morning, Mr. Haas," she said. "I thought
you were in Texas."

She was a very nice woman, but Steve thought that
she simply confirmed his suspicion that the personnel department never hired any women under 50,
and gave preference to grandmothers coming out of
retirement.

"Good morning," Steve said. As he reached the oak
door, it swung open before him, triggered by a button on the receptionist's desk. There was a wide,
bright corridor beyond the door. Three quarters of
the way down it, he passed a door on which was
printed: S. HAAS. So far as offices went, it wasn't much
by any standard, hardly larger than one of the supply
closets, but by the standards of brass hat row, it was
almost a joke. He had once laid on Whitman's desk
a plan drawing, showing quite clearly that there was
more room in Whitman's personal washroom than
behind the door marked S. HAAS. Whitman hadn't
seemed very much amused.

Whitman's office was beyond a heavy plate glass
door opening into a secretary's office.

"Good morning," Steve said. "The boss wants to
see me at nine A.M."

"I'll announce you, Mr. Haas," she said formally.
Normally, she would either make a wisecrack, or
comment on something he had done wrong. Now she
pushed a button on her desk and spoke into the intercom. "Mr. Haas is here, Mr. Whitman."

"Would you ask Mr. Haas to come in, please?" Whitman said, just as formally.

"You can go in, Mr. Haas," the secretary said, as if she thought Steve hadn't been able to hear Whitman's reply.

He pushed open the door to Whitman's office. Whitman was at his desk, his back to an expanse of glass that provided a view of the Detroit Mohave assembly plant, and of Detroit itself.

"Good morning," Steve said.

"Have a nice trip back, did you, Steve?" Mr. Whitman said, and then, before Steve could reply, "You know Mr. Tornell, don't you?"

"No, sir," Steve said. "I don't believe I do."

"Mr. Tornell is with Career Development Branch, Personnel Division," Whitman said.

"Is that so?" Steve said, aware that it wasn't the brightest remark he'd ever made, but also aware that he was expected to say something.

"So this is the elusive Mr. Haas, is it?" Tornell said, beaming brightly, putting out his hand. "How do you do?"

"How do you do?" Steve replied, shaking the hand, wondering what the "elusive" crack was supposed to mean.

"How were things in Texas, Steve?" Whitman asked.

"I was hardly there long enough to form much of an opinion," Steve said, and from the look on Whitman's face, that had been the wrong thing to say. "For a report in a nutshell, those tires may be all right for taxicabs and police cars, but they provide a ride like a truck," Steve amplified, hoping that this is what Whitman wanted him to do.

"I understand you spend a good deal of your time investigating new ideas," Tornell said.

"I sometimes serve as an extra pair of eyes for Mr.

Whitman," Steve said. He was obviously being appraised by this man Tornell, and he didn't much like it.

"How much experience have you had with an assembly plant?"

"None whatever, I'm afraid," Steve said. "I've always been in engineering."

"Engineering has a prominent place in assembly, Mr. Haas," Tornell said, as if correcting Steve.

"Yes, sir, I'm sure it does."

"By and large, Mr. Haas, would you say that you are closely supervised in your duties here in Engineering, or that you have had, by and large, a free hand?"

"I don't know how to answer that," Steve said honestly.

"I'll answer that," Whitman said. "I tell him what to do. I don't often tell him how to do it."

"Thank you, Mr. Whitman," Tornell said, making it politely clear that he would have preferred Steve to answer the question. "He's rather young, you know," he added, speaking to Whitman as if Steve were nowhere around.

"But let us add that he's rather widely experienced," Whitman said.

Curiosity got the best of Steve. "May I ask what this is all about?"

"Your name, Mr. Haas," Tornell said, "has been proposed for a vacancy at the East Point, Georgia, assembly plant, specifically, the assembly line manager position."

"Oh," Steve said. He stole a quick look at Whitman who just perceptibly shook his head, signaling him to keep his mouth shut.

"And I'm here, frankly, to have a look at you."

"I see," Steve said.

"You're a hard man to lay one's hands on," Tornell

said. "I've been trying to have this little chat with you for some time."

"I travel quite a bit," Steve said.

"Then you'd probably welcome a change to spend every night at home for a while, wouldn't you?" Tornell said.

"He's certainly entitled to it," Whitman said, before Steve had a chance to answer.

"Yes, that's been considered," Tornell said. "I wonder, Mr. Haas, if you'd step outside for just a moment?"

"Certainly," Steve said, and got up and left the room, closing the door behind him. Whitman's secretary made it quite clear that she was in no mood for time-killing conversation, and Steve sat down on one of the modernistic sofas, the waiting benches, he called them, and picked up a magazine from the glass and chrome table in front of it.

He didn't have long to wait. Whitman's voice came over the intercom, loud enough for him to hear it: "Would you ask Mr. Haas to step in, please?"

"I heard him," Steve said, getting to his feet before she could repeat the message.

Tornell was smiling broadly, and he had his hand outstretched. "Permit me, Mr. Haas, to be the first to congratulate you on your new appointment."

"Thank you," Steve said.

"Frankly, the way you were recommended, this interview was little more than a formality," Tornell said.

"I see," Steve said.

"As soon as you can break loose here, Mr. Haas," Tornell said. "Check with our Mrs. Nolte, in Personnel Transfers."

"Mrs. Nolte?" Steve repeated.

"Yes, you know her?"

"Nice little old lady, looks like a grandmother?" Steve asked.

"That's right. Not only looks like a grandmother, but is. You do know her?"

"I'm not sure," Steve said, still smiling.

"Well, I'm glad that when we finally had a chance to get together, it was such a pleasant occasion," Tornell said, shaking Steve's hand again, crossing the room to shake Whitman's hand, and then, with a final nod, leaving.

"I didn't know you knew Mrs. Nolte," Whitman said. "I didn't think you'd been inside the Administration Building since the day you came back from Germany."

"I haven't, and I don't know her. It was just another proof of my theory that there is a rule that all female employees have to be at least 55 years old and grandmothers."

Whitman laughed, and then said: "Now, that's hardly the right attitude for the new assembly line manager at East Point."

"I'm glad you brought that up," Steve said wryly. "You want to explain that to me?"

"Not much to explain. There's a vacancy, you were nominated for it, and, frankly, because I have some small weight with the paper pushers, you got it."

"That's very nice, Boss," Steve said. "But there's just one thing. I don't want to go to East Point, Georgia, to be assembly line manager, or anything else."

Whitman looked surprised, and then kept looking at Steve for a full minute without saying anything. Steve returned the stare, half afraid he would start to giggle, as he had when he was a kid and had engaged in a staring match to see who would quit first.

"How old are you, Steve?"

"Twenty-six," Steve said.

"And you've been with the company how long?"

"Three years," he said.

"Counting the year you were in Germany?"

"Yeah."

"And the company wants to make you the Number Three man in a major assembly plant, and you don't want to go?"

"What do I know about assembling cars?"

"That's the point, really," Whitman said. "You're about to learn. You didn't really think you could just stay on here, did you?"

"I formed the idea that that was just what would happen," Steve said.

"You have no ambitions for the future?"

"Sure, I have. I'd like to get into development research, you know that."

"I am, because you are apparently none too bright, going to have to explain some things to you one simple step at a time. You will grant me, won't you, that I am something of an engineer myself?"

"Yes, you are," Steve said, and it wasn't apple polishing but a simple statement of his honest belief when he added, "You're the best engineer in the company."

"Let's say that I am the most *influential* engineer in the company. There are probably a dozen smarter engineers than I am in any one of any of the departments. Smarter, but not nearly so influential. Are you beginning to follow me?"

"I'm not sure," Steve said.

"Let me put it this way. Have you ever wondered why I don't call myself Doctor?"

"Yes, but I figured it was none of my business. Or maybe that you think like I do, that only the medics and the tooth-pullers should use that title."

"Now, I am not at all embarrassed about my Ph.D.," Whitman said. "But I long ago learned around here that among the brass Ph.D. equals egg-head, and egghead equals somebody who doesn't know much about business. Now, are you beginning to follow me?"

"I think so, a little, anyway."

"I got this job, and the jobs that led up to it, particularly, I would say, my job as Chief, Power Plant Engineering, not so much because I was qualified for it as an engineer, but because the executive committee, who makes the decisions, thought of me as Good Ol' Stu Whitman, who ran the Indiana transmission plant, rather than Doctor Stuart Whitman, Ph.D. slip-stick jockey."

"Through the dark of morning," Steve said, starting to smile, "come the first rays of the sun."

"I didn't think you were really that dense," Whitman said.

"You better wait until you explain to me what all this has got to do with me going to Georgia."

"I'll put it in terms you'll understand, sarge," Whitman said, not unkindly. "Who gets promoted in the Army, the platoon sergeant, or the clerk? The battalion commander, or the morale officer?"

"OK," Steve said. "I agree. The commander gets the promotions."

"The same thing applies here at AMC," Whitman said. "Our business has three sides to it. Designing the cars, manufacturing, and selling. Your talent, like mine, is obviously in engineering, or design. I think you would be a lousy salesman, as I would, both because of your personality and because your mind is trained to find weaknesses and things that can be improved, rather than to believe that any particular car or truck is the greatest thing to come off the assembly line since the Dodge Brothers sold Henry Ford his first engines and chassis."

Steve shrugged his shoulders and nodded in agreement. He knew that he could never be a salesman.

"So that leaves manufacturing. If you stayed in engineering, especially here at sort of the top of the engineering heap, you would eventually be shunted into a corner. Engineers, I have learned, are all right 'in their place.' But the decision-making process should be left to those with experience in the cold, cruel world of reality. Do you think I could have gotten half as much money as I did for non-petrocarbon engine research if it had been simply the wild idea of an engineer?" He went on without giving Steve a chance to answer. "I got that money because they believed me, in the Administration Building, when I said that it would be an eventual source of profit for us. Because I'd been, in other words, a member of the manufacturing team for a long time and couldn't be considered, on the basis of past performance, as some wild-eyed mad scientist."

"You're telling me that if I expect to get promoted, really promoted, I have to get the same sort of experience, right? And hopefully the same sort of reputation?"

"Exactly, Steve," Whitman said. "There's a great deal of satisfaction, not to mention the money, in being in a decision-making position. And while I think you're a good engineer, I think you're a doer, too. That you could do a better job for the company, and for yourself, if you could work yourself into a job where you had the responsibility for directing other people."

"If I'd known you felt this way, I would have bought a bigger hat," Steve said.

Whitman chuckled. "That's something else you're going to have to learn, Steve, or maybe forget is the better word. You're going to have to learn to act like a relatively senior engineer, not like some sergeant we hired off the street. You're not going to be able to crack wise to your boss at East Point, or for that matter, to the people who'll be working for you."

"Old Sobersides?" Steve asked.

"Precisely," Whitman said.

"How long am I going to have to stay at East Point?"

"Couple of years, maybe three," Whitman said. "You're awfully young to get the job in the first place, as Tornell carefully pointed out. Before you're eligible for another promotion, you're going to have to be older. Or at least give the brass the impression, based on the facts, of maturity. I'd like to have you back here, but that may be a hard thing to accomplish. At least, any time soon."

"Can I ask a question?"

"Shoot."

"Why did you go to all this trouble for me?"

"You didn't do it on purpose, I'm sure, but you paid me the greatest compliment."

"I don't quite understand you."

"Imitation is the sincerest form of flattery," Whitman said. "You think like I do, you act like I do, and it's very pleasing to find that one is not the only nut in the world."

"Well," Steve said. "I appreciate it, Stu, I really do. But I don't know about East Point. I'm liable to be way over my head."

"Just keep, in that tired Army cliché, your eyes and ears open and your mouth shut," Whitman said, "and you'll be all right. Learn as much as you can, Steve, about everything, and I mean everything. Here, you've seen from the top, looking down. Now, you're going to get the other view, from the bottom so to speak, looking up."

"When do I go?" Steve asked.

"Just as soon as you're ready. If you'd like a little

vacation before you report, a week or ten days, that can be arranged."

"That would be like putting off a visit to the dentist," Steve said. "But how about finishing up the tire tests in Texas, first?"

"I'm going to run down there myself," Whitman said.

Steve nodded. It would apparently be a long time before he got to see that good-looking girl in Dallas again.

At ten thirty, he presented himself at the desk of Mrs. Nolte, in the Personnel Transfers section of the Personnel Division. In the time between his leaving Whitman's office until he'd gone across the plant area to the Administration Building, he'd made up his mind.

First, he'd rejected the idea that he would just quit, rather than go to East Point. For one thing, being transferred wasn't much different from the Army; the Army never asked you if you wanted a transfer, and no one was ever permitted to say no. For another, he had long before learned that everything, good things as well as bad ones, always had to come to an end. He had for two years been paid for having a ball; now it was time to do something he didn't want to do in exchange for his paycheck.

Whitman was right, of course, about what would have happened to him if he had just stayed around here. Whitman had a rather unique talent for being right about most things. If he ever was to get in a position where he really could do something himself, rather than as an extension of Whitman, he was going to have to play the game by the rules. The way to do that was to follow Whitman's and the Army's key to success: Keeping his eyes and his ears open and his mouth shut.

"My name is Haas," he said to Mrs. Nolte. "Mr.

Tornell suggested that I see you about my transfer to East Point."

"Frankly I expected a somewhat older man," Mrs. Nolte said. "You are to be congratulated, Mr. Haas."

"Thank you," Steve said.

"Please sit down, Mr. Haas," she said, "and we'll get under way."

Mrs. Nolte was more than a little surprised, among other things, to learn that she would not have to arrange with a mover for the transfer of his household goods, for the simple reason that he didn't have any.

"I presume that you will be driving your car," she said. "The company will reimburse you for your car's use at the rate of sixteen cents per mile." She consulted a company book which had the official distance in miles between Detroit and East Point.

"I don't have a car, I'm afraid," Steve said, and then added, thinking aloud, "I'll have to get one."

"In that case, you would have the option of travel by air, either on a company plane, or commercially, and we would, of course, reimburse you for any extra baggage weight."

"I'll get a car," Steve decided. He would need one when he got there, anyway. Mrs. Nolte arranged for several checks. He would be paid until the end of the month by the Engineering Division, and after the first by the East Point Assembly. He got another check for the mileage, and a third check for his expenses en route.

When he'd finished with Mrs. Nolte, he went back to see if Whitman would have dinner with him, only to learn that Whitman was already off to Texas. He was more than a little disappointed, but it seemed to make it official that he was no longer errand boy to the Vice President, Engineering.

Whitman's secretary got him a company car to

carry off what few personal possessions he had in his office. There weren't many. As the car carried him toward Detroit, he changed the directions he'd given the driver.

"How about taking me to a rental car agency, instead?" Steve asked.

The rental agency had a fine-looking, bright yellow Ford convertible for hire, but Steve, following his new role as a sobersided employee, and considering that after all, Amalgamated was paying for it, rented a standard four-door Amalgamated Mohawk sedan.

It took him thirty minutes to load his clothes, and the two guns, and the picture of his mother into the Mohawk. He gave Ernie, the bellhop, the contents of the refrigerator, shook his hand, and drove away.

CHAPTER THREE

STEVE'S NEW-FOUND resolve to go strictly by the book lasted until four that afternoon. He'd made good time on the Interstate, and was obviously going to make Atlanta long before the two-and-a-half-days' travel time established by company policy was up. He did some quick mental figuring, and realized that he would arrive, according to plan, on a Saturday afternoon. No one wanted to greet a new employee on a Saturday afternoon.

He changed superhighways at the next intersection, and drove to Pennsylvania, where he spent a day and a half with his mother, most of it, it seemed, at a table literally groaning under vast amounts of food, and then drove down the Interstate to Atlanta, arriving there on Sunday afternoon.

He found a motel, and then drove to East Point.

Finding the assembly plant itself wasn't difficult. It was a 150-acre industrial site, fenced in, with a vast expanse of grass and a huge sign, featuring the most elegant model of the Mohawk line, the Warrior station wagon, about five times life size.

Steve could see several hundred new cars, of all sizes and colors, parked in neat rows, but there seemed to be no activity in the plant, and the security guards had closed three of the four lanes at the main entrance with the sliding gate.

On the way back to the motel, he saw signs pointing to the Atlanta International Speedway. He followed them, in the faint hope that there would be racing, but the track parking lot was deserted, and he saw on a huge signboard that the next races would be the following week.

He went back to the motel, and ate the Family Sunday Smorgasbord, feeling a little uneasy alone with all the families and the hordes of kids. He spent Sunday evening watching television in his room.

When he got to the plant at half-past eight Monday morning, the sliding gate at the main entrance had been fully opened, and a steady stream of traffic was moving in and out.

As he drove past the gate, the guard, who had been simply waving people through, put up his hand, and then, when Steve didn't stop quickly enough, blew his whistle. Steve stopped and then rolled down the window as the security guard walked up.

"Where you headed?"

"For the office," Steve said. "Do I need a pass or something?"

"Yes, sir," the guard said, and Steve wasn't particularly pleased with the way he said it. "Pull over there and then come back to the guard shack." He pointed to a parking space.

"You ever try saying 'please'?" Steve asked.

"Please," the security guard said, thickly sarcastic. Steve nodded and parked the rented car where he was directed, then got out and walked to the guard shack.

"Now," the guard said, "where is it exactly you want to go?"

"Do you always provide this sort of warm welcome to strangers?" Steve asked, now more than a little annoyed. "Or am I getting special treatment?"

"It's as simple as this, buddy," the guard said. "You tell me where you want to go, and then I find out if I can let you go on. OK?"

"I want to go to the office of the plant's assembly line manager," Steve said.

"That's more like it," the guard said. "What's your name?"

"Haas," Steve said. "Aich Double-A Ess."

"And what's the nature of your business with the assembly line manager, Mr. Haas?"

"You have to know that, too?" Steve asked. "Is that a plant policy?"

"That's right."

"I'm reporting for work," Steve said.

"Well, then, let's see your Notice to Report for Employment," the guard said.

"I don't have one," Steve said. "But if you'll call up there, I think they'll tell you that I'm expected."

"You don't have the form?" the guard said, and then, when Steve shook his head, said: "You're supposed to bring it with you."

"How about calling up?" Steve said. "Just out of the goodness of your heart?"

"Let me give you a word of advice," the guard said. "With an attitude like that, you're not going to last long around here."

"Call up," Steve said flatly.

Taking his time about it, the security guard found

a plant telephone book, took some time to find the number, and then dialed it. When it began to ring, he handed it to Steve.

A feminine voice came on the line: "Mr. Chennowith's office."

"Is this the assembly line manager's office?" Steve asked.

"Yes, it is."

"My name is Haas," Steve said. "I'm at the main gate, and I can't get the guard to let me in."

"Oh?"

"I don't have my Notice to Report for Employment," Steve added helpfully.

"Let me speak to him," the voice said. Steve handed the telephone to the guard.

"She wants to talk to you," Steve said.

Thirty seconds later, somewhat reluctantly, the guard hung up the telephone and wrote out a pass and handed it to Steve. "She says it's all right to let you pass," he said.

"Thank you," Steve said. "This warm welcome has really touched me."

The guard just gave him a dirty look.

Steve got back in the rented car and drove to the administration building. In front of the building, small signs had been put up identifying individual parking spaces. Three of them said "visitor" and Steve stopped before one of these. As he got out of the car and walked toward the dual plate glass doors to the building, he saw that other spaces were reserved for the General Manager, the Director of Administration, Director of Purchasing, Transportation Manager and Assembly Line Manager. A car, in each case a Mohawk, was parked in front of each sign, including the Assembly Line Manager's sign.

Inside the building, a receptionist sat at a large

desk. This time it was an attractive young woman whose smile seemed genuine.

"Good morning," she said. "May I help you?"

"I'd like to see the General Manager, please," Steve said. "My name is Haas."

"Have you an appointment, Mr. Haas?"

"I'm afraid not," Steve said. "But I think he expects me."

"Just one moment, please," she said, and she picked up a telephone, dialed a number, and told someone that Mr. Haas was here to see Mr. Pickens. Steve couldn't hear the other end of the conversation, but the announcement had apparently caused some surprise, because the receptionist added: "Yes, standing right here in the lobby." There was another reply to this, and in a moment the receptionist said, "Right down the corridor, Mr. Haas, the fifth door to your right."

Steve followed directions, and pushed open a door to find a room identical to any one of twenty rooms in either the Engineering Building or the Administration Building in Detroit. Executive offices at Amalgamated were apparently stamped out like the cars on the assembly line, differing only in small detail from one another. The general manager here, Steve quickly saw, obviously did not rank as high in the corporate pecking order as Stu Whitman. His office reflected this. It was nice, but it was not very elegant. It looked more like the office of a high school principal than anything else.

"You're Mr. Haas?" his secretary, a gray-haired woman in her late forties, said, making it more of a statement than a question.

"Yes, ma'am," Steve said.

The secretary pushed a button on her intercom. "Mr. Haas is here, Mr. Pickens."

"Send him in," a male voice said, and she waved

Steve toward an interior door. As Steve opened it, it was tugged inward by someone on the inside. He found himself facing a tall, balding man with a full set of white teeth.

"I'm Larry Pickens, Mr. Haas," he said. "Come on in, and we'll see if we can't get this straightened out."

"How do you do?" Steve said, shaking the hand Pickens offered.

"I'm really very sorry about this," Pickens said. Steve thought that Pickens was making reference to the trouble he had had getting in the plant.

"No lasting harm done," he said. "I did get past the gate, after all."

Pickens looked at him with a look that seemed to be mingled annoyance and confusion.

"The heart of the problem, Haas," he said, waving Steve into a seat, "is that I took three weeks vacation. Nineteen years with Amalgamated, and the first time I've ever had off more than five days at a time."

Steve had no idea how Pickens taking a vacation could have anything to do with a surly, unfriendly security guard, but he decided the best thing to do was keep his mouth shut and see what happened.

"And then, the first thing this morning, when I got here, I learned for the first time about all this." He looked at Steve and added, "There's nothing personal in this, you realize."

"I think," Steve said, "that you'd better explain what you mean, Mr. Pickens. I'm afraid I haven't been following you."

"Oh," Pickens said thoughtfully. Then: "I'm very much afraid that your trip here has been a, well, rather a wild goose chase, Mr. Haas. The point is, we have an assembly line manager."

"Apparently, nobody told Detroit," Steve said. "They sent me here for that job."

"Well, that's where the confusion apparently begins," Pickens said. "Here, let me show you. It's dated almost a month ago."

He handed Steve a carbon copy of a Telex message:

FROM AMC ASSEMBLY PLANT 15 EAST POINT GA
TO VICE PRESIDENT PERSONNEL ADMINISTRATIVE
BUILDING AMC DETROIT

ROBERT B. CHENNOWITH, ASSISTANT MANAGER, ASSEMBLY LINE, WAS APPOINTED TO BE MANAGER ASSEMBLY LINE EFFECTIVE TODAY TO FILL VACANCY CREATED BY EARLY RETIREMENT OF CLAUDE B. DEMMECK. IT IS RECOMMENDED THAT MR. CHENNOWITH BE ADVANCED TO CATEGORY 22 WITH FURTHER ADVANCEMENT TO CATEGORY 20 FOLLOWING SUCCESSFUL COMPLETION OF PROBATIONARY ASSIGNMENT.

LAWRENCE PICKENS, GENERAL MANAGER

"I see," Steve said, after he'd read it and handed it back.

"Some fool clerk out there misplaced it, is all I can figure," Pickens said. "Because when I got here this morning, there was this." He handed Steve a Telex message form:

FROM VICE PRESIDENT PERSONNEL AMC DETROIT
TO GENERAL MANAGER ASSEMBLY PLANT 15 EAST
POINT GA

STEFAN B. HAAS CATEGORY 20 WILL REPORT DURING NEXT TEN DAYS AS MANAGER ASSEMBLY LINE. FOLLOWING PROBATIONARY ASSIGNMENT YOU ARE AUTHORIZED TO ADVANCE HAAS TO CATEGORY 18.

JEROME B. TORNELL FOR VICE PRESIDENT
ADMINISTRATION

"I realize this puts you in an unfortunate position, Mr. Haas," Pickens said.

"Let's say I'm sort of confused."

"Now, what I've done, Haas, is send another Telex," Pickens said. "Before you got here this morning." He handed still another Telex message to Steve:

FROM AMC ASSEMBLY PLANT 15 EAST POINT GA
TO VICE PRESIDENT, PERSONNEL ADMINISTRATIVE
BUILDING AMC DETROIT

REFERENCE YOUR MESSAGE RE: HAAS SIGNED TORNELL. FURTHER REFERENCE MY TELEX RE: ROBERT B. CHENNOWITH. CHENNOWITH HAS BEEN PROMOTED ASSEMBLY LINE MANAGER EFFECTIVE 6 JUNE AND NO VACANCY EXISTS HERE. FOR YOUR FURTHER INFORMATION, HOWARD G. COLE HAS BEEN NAMED ASSISTANT MANAGER TO FILL CHENNOWITH VACANCY.

LAWRENCE PICKENS, GENERAL MANAGER

"It looks like I'm a member of the Army of the Unemployed," Steve said.

"No, since it's their mistake, I'm sure the whole thing will shortly be straightened out," Pickens said. "I really don't think they'll put you out on the street."

As if on cue, the intercom spoke: "Mr. Pickens, Mr. Tornell is on the line."

"Put him through," Pickens said eagerly, and then to Steve, "I'll put it on the loudspeaker, so that you'll be in on this."

He pushed a button on a small box by his telephone, and then said, "Hello, Mr. Tornell, Larry Pickens here."

"I just got your Telex," Tornell's familiar voice said.

"What did you fellas do out there, misplace my first Telex?"

"I have before me," Tornell's nasal voice said, "a carbon of our Telex to you dated 6 June. Shall I read it to you? Since it has been apparently misplaced there?"

"I think perhaps you'd better," Pickens said.

"Very well," Tornell said. "Quote. The position of Manager, Assembly Line, at all plants was placed within assignment jurisdiction of Vice President, Personnel, effective 1 January this year. All plants were so notified by Telex, same subject, 20 December last year. Consequently, since the retirement of Mr. Demmeck, Personnel has been in the process of reviewing records of all eligible personnel to fill his vacancy. No decision has been reached. For your information, Mr. Chennowith is one of those under consideration. Please advise Mr. Chennowith that no decision has been reached." There was a pause. "Unquote." Tornell went on. "I signed the Telex."

"I can't begin to suggest what might have happened," Pickens said. "But I told Chennowith that he's been promoted."

"I'm sorry," Tornell said. "He didn't get the job."

"I'm going to have to protest, Mr. Tornell," Pickens said. "Most vigorously."

"Just between you and me, Pickens," Tornell said, "you'll be a small voice crying in the wilderness. You're getting a fair-haired boy named Haas. One of the problems making appointments at this level, obviously, is that the upper echelon brass always seem to have a fair-haired boy, as well as the ear of the Chairman of the Board. In this case, you were up against Stuart Whitman, and Whitman won. It's as simple as that. I wasn't even asked, really, to be more than a rubber stamp in the whole affair."

"I see," Pickens said, and his face whitened.

"It should make your day complete when Haas actually arrives," Tornell said. "He's been with the company all of three years, and doesn't look like he's old enough to vote. On the other hand, Whitman, who normally doesn't do this sort of thing, seems to feel that he has a great deal of potential. In any case, it's academic. You've got Haas, and that's all there is to it."

"I don't want to sound argumentative, Mr. Tornell," Pickens said. "But I feel that I have to carry this further. Specifically, I'm going to discuss it with the Vice President, Personnel."

"I brought this matter to his attention before calling you, Mr. Pickens," Tornell said. "He has given you authorization to advance Mr. Chennowith to Category 22, as assistant assembly line manager, and he asked me to ask you to tell Mr. Chennowith that he will be given every consideration for promotion the next time a suitable vacancy occurs."

"You're telling me that a man with sixteen years with the company, obviously highly qualified for the job, is to lose it to someone with three years with the company?" Pickens said.

"Yes, I'm afraid I am," Tornell said. "That decision has been made."

"I intend to pursue the matter further," Pickens said.

"That, of course, is your privilege," Tornell said. "But in the meantime, when Haas gets there, in the absence of further direction from here, he is the assembly line manager."

"Good morning, Mr. Tornell," Pickens said, icily polite. "Thank you for calling." He pushed the button on the telephone again, and then spun around in his chair, face white, to stare out his window.

Finally, he turned the chair again to face Steve.

"I'm sorry you heard that conversation," he said. "That wasn't a wise move on my part."

"Mr. Pickens," Steve said, "I think you should know I didn't ask for this job. I was brought back from Texas and told I would take it."

"I wonder if that will make Mr. Chennowith feel any better?" Pickens said. Then: "How much assembly line experience do you have?"

"None whatever," Steve said. "I've been in development since I came with the company."

"And before that?"

"I went to college. And before that, I was in the Army."

"And do you think you're qualified to take over the assembly line here?"

"No, I don't," Steve said. "And I told Mr. Whitman and Mr. Tornell that I knew nothing about it."

"What you do, Haas, in a situation like this, when you're convinced that upper level management has suddenly gone mad, is to remind yourself of two things. First, that they are upper level management, and entitled to the benefit of the doubt, and second, that you are, after all, an employee, and supposed to take orders."

"Yes, sir," Steve said.

"What you have to do," Pickens said, as much to himself as to Steve, "is convince yourself that there is a reason for it, a bona fide, logical reason for it." He looked at Steve, and when Steve made no reply, said: "Well, putting it off isn't going to do anyone any good." He pushed a button on his intercom: "Bob," he said. "Are you there?"

"Just got in, Larry," a pleasant male voice said. "Got stuck in traffic. Something?"

"Would you come in for a moment, right away, please, Bob?" Pickens said.

"On my way."

"Mr. Haas," Pickens said, "the assembly line manager's office is at the end of this corridor. Would you be good enough to go there and wait for me?"

"Yes, sir," Steve said.

He stood up and left Pickens' office. As he walked down the corridor to the end of the building, he passed a man coming the other way. He was a tall, rather stout, pleasant-faced man, with just a touch of gray at his temples. He looked like he had been an athlete in his youth. He smiled at Steve as they passed. Steve stopped in the corridor long enough to see him enter Pickens' office, and then pushed open the door marked: "MANAGER, ASSEMBLY LINE."

A good-looking redhead, with freckles, looked up from her typewriter.

"Good morning," she said. "Can I help you?"

"I'm ... uh ... waiting to see Mr. Pickens," Steve said.

"This is Mr. Chennowith's office," the redhead said.

"Yes, I know," Steve said.

"May I ask your name?" she said, obviously confused.

"Haas," Steve said, sitting down on a small couch and reaching for a magazine, more to have something to do with his hands than to have something to read.

"You're the gentleman who called from the gate?"

"Yes, I am," Steve said.

"I ... uh," she said nervously, "I presumed that when you called here, you had an appointment with Mr. Chennowith," she said. "But I asked Mr. Chennowith, and he knew nothing about you."

"I think Mr. Chennowith will be here in just a few minutes," Steve said. "I know Mr. Pickens will be."

"Then you do have business with Mr. Chennowith?" she asked.

"Yes, I guess I do," Steve said.

"Well, at least I won't have to call security," she said. "Mr. Chennowith said that if you didn't show up here, I was to call security."

"What I really am," Steve said, "is a spy. I'm here to steal the secret of the atom bomb."

She didn't think that was especially funny. "Would you care to tell me whom you represent, Mr. Haas?" she said. "So that I can announce you when Mr. Chennowith returns?"

"I'm with the company," Steve said.

"May I ask where?"

"Right here, Red," Steve said. "Relax. I'm perfectly legitimate."

She obviously didn't like being called "Red," either. She turned to her typewriter and began to type very rapidly.

It was fifteen minutes before Pickens, followed by Chennowith, the man Steve had passed in the hall, came through the door. Steve had fifteen minutes to carefully consider the fix he was in, and to search, desperately but wholly unsuccessfully, for some possible alternative.

CHAPTER FOUR

HE GOT TO his feet when he saw Pickens.

The redhead also got up. "This is Mr. Haas, Mr. Chennowith," she said. "He's waiting for Mr. Pickens."

"Yes, I know," Chennowith said. He looked as if he had just been kicked in the stomach, actually pale. But he put a smile on his face, and put out his hand. "How do you do, Mr. Haas?"

Steve thought it would have been easier if Chennowith had been livid with rage, as he had every right in the world to be.

"How do you do, sir?" Steve said. The "sir" came automatically. Steve was long in the habit of calling men some ten or fifteen years his senior "sir." Not only was Chennowith that much older, but he was the sort of man whose very appearance seemed to call for respect.

"Mr. Haas, this is Janet Fallon," Chennowith said.

"How do you do?" Steve said politely.

"How do you do?" the redhead said, and then, apparently deciding that if the boss was going to be civil, she should be civil too, she added: "Are you going to be with us, Mr. Haas?"

"That, Janet," Chennowith said, "is what you can call the understatement of the day."

"I'm sorry?" Janet said.

"Mr. Haas has been appointed assembly line manager," Chennowith said. "He's your new boss."

She looked stricken. "But—what about you?"

"I am to be Mr. Haas's assistant," Chennowith said. "Would you bring us some coffee, please, into Mr. Haas's office?"

Chennowith's—*his*—office wasn't much different from, nor much smaller than, Pickens' office. The assembly line manager was the Number Three man in the assembly plant. The office, in size and furnishings, seemed to reflect that. Steve would have been uncomfortable seeing it for the first time, even if there had been no confusion about Chennowith.

Chennowith almost ostentatiously sat at one of two armchairs in the room, rather than behind the desk with the sign ROBERT CHENNOWITH sitting on it. Pickens sat down on the couch against the wall. Steve, uncomfortably, sat down in the other armchair.

"I've explained to Mr. Chennowith what has transpired," Pickens said. "And he was present when I put in a telephone call to the Vice President, Personnel, and explained my position in the matter."

When Steve had nothing to say to that, Pickens went on. "You have been confirmed, or perhaps I should say, re-confirmed, as the assembly line manager, Mr. Haas. So we're going to proceed from there."

Steve nodded. He really could think of nothing to say.

The redhead appeared with a tray, bearing three plastic insulated cups of coffee. Pointedly, Steve thought, he got his last, but she did ask: "How do you take your coffee, Mr. Haas?"

"Black, please," Steve said. There was no conversation until she left.

"I think the best thing for me to do," Pickens said, as if he had just made up his mind, "is to leave you two alone. My door's always open to you, Mr. Haas."

"Thank you," Steve said.

"Take whatever time you need to get settled, of course. Mr. Chennowith is wholly capable of handling assembly in your absence."

"Thank you," Steve said again. "I'm sure he is."

Pickens got up, nodded to both of them and left.

Steve met Chennowith's eyes. "I have a strange urge to apologize," Steve said. "But the fact is, I'm not responsible for this."

"I've thought of that," Chennowith said.

"I wonder why the Telex from Personnel never got here," Steve said, "the one saying the job was to be filled by Personnel rather than by Mr. Pickens."

"I'm sure it did come," Chennowith said. "I think Pickens tried to get me the job anyway, and lost."

"I thought that's maybe what happened," Steve said. "This leaves you holding the short end of the stick, though, doesn't it?"

"I got the raise. I've been trying to tell myself that the money is what counts. And it does help," Chennowith said. "I don't think that will give my wife much satisfaction, though. Women seem interested as much in status as anything else." Then, quickly, he added: "I don't think I should have said that. I don't want to whimper."

"I think, in your shoes, I would be howling with rage," Steve said. "Blame it on me, if you like. I don't mind being the bad guy. I've no wife to consider."

Chennowith looked up at him from his coffee cup, very thoughtfully. "The first thing you think of, of course, is quitting, telling the company where to head in. But it's not quite that simple. Not if you have a large mortgage and kids in school. What you think about is what you'd be giving up. In my case, that would be a lot of money and sixteen years. I would like to know, if you don't mind my asking, how you came to get the job."

"Tornell put it rather bluntly," Steve said. "He called me a fair-haired boy. Until last week, I worked for Stuart Whitman. Whitman apparently got me the job. I wasn't asked if I wanted it; I was told I was getting it."

"It's quite a step up," Chennowith said. "It calls for a Category 22."

"I was a 22. They've made me a 20," Steve said.

"You were already a 22?"

"I think that was more to show who I worked for than anything else," Steve said.

"Well, I'll tell you frankly, Mr. Haas," Chennowith said. "What I decided, in Pickens' office, after I decided I couldn't afford to quit to salve a damaged ego, was that somebody high in the company apparently feels that you can do the job. If I accept that, and I think I should, then the only thing for me to do is to tell you that I'm here to help. Just tell me how I can do that, Mr. Haas, and we'll go on from there."

"You can start by calling me 'Steve,' " Steve said. "If you would."

Chennowith put his hand out. "Welcome to Assembly Plant Number Fifteen, Steve," he said.

"Thank you," Steve said.

"Where do we start?" Chennowith said.

"The first thing we have to worry about is your assistant, who apparently is no longer the assistant assembly line manager," Steve said. "How's he going to react to this?"

"Not well, I'm afraid," Chennowith said. "It's even worse with him. He's an older fellow. Worked his way up from the line."

"Older than you?"

"Yes."

"Great," Steve said sarcastically.

"Are you open to suggestion?"

"Wide open," Steve replied.

"I don't know how Pickens would react to this, but you could make him assistant in charge of night and overtime operations. Then, maybe, if he was able to keep his pay raise, it wouldn't burn so much."

"Is he here today?"

"No. He generally takes Monday off. He comes in on Sunday for a couple of hours, both to check the special orders assembled, and to check in in-flow of components."

Steve had only a vague idea of what that meant, but at least it gave him a little time.

"Is there an intercom, or something, on which I could talk to Pickens?" he asked.

"On my desk," Chennowith said, then, immediately: "On *your* desk. I'll show you."

They walked to the desk, and Chennowith pointed out one switch, of about a dozen, that would put Steve in touch with Pickens. Steve pushed it.

"Mr. Pickens?" he said.

"Yes?"

"This is Haas, Mr. Pickens," he said. "I've been thinking about Mr. Cole."

"Have you?"

"Under the circumstances, I'd like to change his title, and see that he keeps his pay raise."

"Go on."

"I'd like to name him assistant manager for night operations, or something like that, and be able to tell him that what's happened isn't going to affect his pay raise."

"The point, Haas," Pickens said, "is that doing that would create another upper management slot. I don't think our management budget will permit that."

"I think, under the circumstances, it's important," Steve said.

"But the decision is mine, Mr. Haas, and I don't concur. Is there anything else?"

"Not right now," Steve said. "Thank you." He flipped the lever up, and looked at Chennowith. "Now what?"

"I don't really know," Chennowith said. "But mine not to reason why—"

"Yeah," Steve said. "But he won't be in until to-morrow?"

"No. Are you settled, by any chance?"

"No. And I've got to get a rental car returned, and find someplace to live, too."

"I'm not trying to get rid of you, Steve, but why don't you take the rest of the day off and get settled? That'll give me a chance to get the desk cleaned out, and maybe I'll be able to think of something for Cole."

Steve flipped the intercom lever again. "Mr. Pickens, with your permission, I'd like to take the rest of the day off and get settled."

"By all means," Pickens said. "Take as long as you want. We want you to be happy here, Mr. Haas." His tone was right on the edge of sarcasm.

"Thank you very much," Steve said. He had just

formed an unpleasant opinion. What was making Pickens difficult was not because Steve had bumped Chennowith out of a promotion, but because Pickens' authority had been challenged. If he had been willing, out of loyalty to Chennowith, to telephone the Vice President, Personnel, it would seem logical that he'd do what he could to soften the blow for Cole, too.

Steve sat thinking about this for a moment, and then had another idea, at a tangent.

"Isn't there a company policy that you can buy a car at a discount?"

"Certainly," Chennowith said. Then he smiled. "You don't mean to tell me you're not driving a Mohawk?"

"I'm driving a rented one," Steve said. "I never had to own one before. A fringe benefit."

"Open for another suggestion?" Chennowith asked.

"Sure. Don't even bother to ask," Steve said.

"Tomorrow, or whenever you come in, why don't you follow your car through assembly? I mean, we'll set up a special order computer card, and you can watch the whole business, from beginning to end. If you'd like, I'll have Janet type up a purchase requisition for Mr. Pickens' signature. When are you planning on coming back?"

"Tomorrow morning," Steve said. "I think Cole is entitled to learn the bad news from me."

"Would you do that for me?" Chennowith said. "I'd appreciate it."

"Be glad to."

"Any idea what kind of car you want?" Chennowith said.

"Four wheels and an engine," Steve said. "A cheap one." Chennowith nodded, and then Steve changed his mind. "Wait a minute. Let's show the proper team spirit. A Warrior convertible, with every option we sell."

"OK," Chennowith said, and he smiled. "I'll make it up and have it in Pickens' office so that it will be back by the time you are."

"Thank you," Steve said. "Now I'm going to get out of here."

"See you tomorrow," Chennowith said. But, just as Steve was going out the door, he called his name again and Steve turned to see that he was holding out a paperbound book to him. "I don't know if you'll have the time to read this," he said, "but it might help."

Steve took the book. It was a typewritten manuscript, reproduced on a copying machine. The title was: *Duties, Authorities & Responsibilities of Assembly Line Manager, Plant Number Fifteen.*

"I never finished reading it myself," Chennowith said. "But you might find it interesting."

"Thanks," Steve said, and finally left. At Janet Fallon's desk, he stopped.

"Miss Fallon, would you be good enough to telephone the gate and arrange with whoever's in charge for permission for me to get in and out of this place?"

"Certainly, Mr. Haas," she said, icily polite.

"I had an awful time getting in," Steve said. "Remember?"

"Is that so?" she asked, almost nastily, and certainly coldly.

Steve looked at her a moment. It seemed strange, since Chennowith was apparently a nice guy going along with a bad situation. that she should act like this. On the other hand, loyalty to Chennowith was obviously behind it, and you could hardly jump on her for that.

"I'll be in at about eight in the morning, Miss Fallon," he said. "I don't know where I can be reached until then, but if I find someplace to live, I'll call in."

"I'm sure that Mr. Chennowith can handle things in your absence, Mr. Haas," she said, and flashed him an icy smile. Then she picked up the telephone, effectively shutting off any other attempts to make friends.

When he got in his car, he looked at his watch. It was twenty-five past ten, and that surprised him. He had thought it was much later. Well, a lot had happened in the not quite two hours he'd been inside.

The same guard who had given him the trouble when he entered the plant flagged him down as he started to pass through the gate.

"I thought Miss Fallon had arranged for me to get in and out," Steve said, after he'd rolled down the window.

"She called, Mr. Haas," the guard said. "But—now don't get mad at me—the policy is that you'll have to have this signed either by somebody in personnel, or by one of the big shots." He handed Steve a printed form.

"Do they consider the assembly line manager a big shot?" Steve asked.

"He'd do just fine," the guard said. "Sorry to have to send you back inside."

"You won't have to," Steve said, and for the first time, he signed "S. Haas, Asmbly. Line Mgr."

"Oh," the guard said, when he saw it. "I didn't know, Mr. Haas." He was now subdued.

The sergeant flared in Steve. Just in time, he bit off, "You should have asked," and said, instead, "You had no way of knowing."

It would have been cheap and meaningless, Steve knew, to jump all over the guard. He was no longer a sergeant, and permitted to change things by jumping all over people on the spot. The way to handle this was to pass it downward through channels. Have someone in personnel tell someone in the Security Force to suggest that courtesy on the part of the gate guards wasn't all that it should be, and would they pay a little more attention to it, please?

He drove toward Atlanta, returned to his motel, and bought a newspaper in the lobby. He checked the classified ads for furnished apartments, was shocked at the prices asked, and then checked the unfurnished apartments.

He was going to have to start behaving like a civilized human being, rather than a sergeant on temporary duty somewhere. He was half pleased with himself, and half embarrassed, when he corrected himself: He was going to have to start behaving like a civilized *executive.*

That meant an apartment, with furniture. A decent apartment, one to which he could bring people, much as Whitman and the others had brought him, for an evening of business conducted in a "social" atmosphere.

One advertisement caught his eye. *"Forest Wood,"* it read. *"Garden Apartments of Distinction. Pool. Tennis. Putting Green."*

"Well, la de da da," Steve said aloud. He was amused at the picture of himself on a putting green. But then other words in the advertisement caught his eye. *"Maid service available. 24-hour telephone answering service. Single bedroom apartments from $185."*

That was just about a hundred dollars a month more than he had paid at the D'Arcy Residential Hotel in Detroit. He considered the price outrageous, but the Forest Wood Garden Apartments kept popping into his mind as he looked at the other apartments in the paper. Methodically, he circled five different apartments which seemed to show some promise, and actually went and looked at two of them. The prospect of living in either of them scared him. They were ugly, for one thing, and worse, the other tenants seemed to have a dozen small children each. And they were not the sort of place to which the assembly line manager of Assembly Point Number 15 could bring guests.

It wouldn't hurt, he decided, just to take a look at Forest Wood. It was some distance from the plant, but it was near the superhighway, and getting to the plant wouldn't take any longer on the superhighway than going through Atlanta streets.

He found the rental office, and even before he saw the apartments available, had decided to take one. The rental office window opened on the interior of the building, which contained the tennis court. Gathered around the tennis court were at least a dozen attractive young women in bathing suits.

"Many of our tenants are stewardesses and other airline people," the rental office manager said.

"Is that so?" Steve said, and for the first time that day, he smiled broadly. There was a one-bedroom apartment available, but he turned it down in favor of a two-bedroom apartment whose windows just happened to overlook the pool. He reasoned that if he could afford $185 for a single-bedroom apartment, just to have some place to entertain business guests, it was perfectly logical to pay $235 for a better apartment with a splendid view of the great outdoors and the creatures of nature.

He winced a little as he wrote out a check for the first month's rent, and for a $200 deposit against breakage, but reinforced his good intentions by having another look at the swimming creatures of nature.

Then he got in the rented car and drove to downtown Atlanta. The die had been cast, and now he would need furniture. On the way downtown, he felt very chipper. The one thing wrong with a hotel bed was that it really wasn't large enough for someone of his bulk. Now, finally, he would be able to have a good-sized bed of his own. If he was going at all, he might as well go first class.

By the time he reached the department store, he had decided that he would also buy a large, man-sized armchair, with a footrest. Price would be no object.

The good feeling lasted through the purchase of the king-sized bed and mattress and box spring. He learned that the price of such luxury items did not increase in direct proportion to the increase in size, but almost geometrically. He had had no idea at all that a bed could cost that much, but he gritted his teeth and gave the order. He next bought a chair, with the same reaction of not having before had any idea how much a good chair could cost. But he made the mistake of sitting down in a chair described by the salesman as "the latest thing," and realized that it was the most comfortable chair he had ever been in.

"I'll take it," he said. "Can I have it delivered to-day?"

"Oh, I don't think that will be possible," the salesman said.

"Well, then," Steve said, "forget it. I'll have to find some store that will deliver it today. I need some place to lie down and sit down."

"I'm sure we can make an exception, sir," the salesman said quickly.

Before he left the store, he found out that the sheets for king-sized beds were priced as the beds themselves were priced. Paying for them finally killed every last urge to spend money. He now resolved to furnish the rest of the apartment with used furniture.

Then he went back to Forest Wood, and into his absolutely bare apartment. He unloaded the car, hung his clothing up, leaned his rifle and his shotgun in opposite corners of the living room, and settled down to wait for the bed and chair to be delivered. He was convinced that the best place to wait was down by the pool, where he could enjoy the benefits of nature.

It was only after he had changed into swimming trunks that he realized he didn't own a towel. He put his clothes back on over his trunks and went shopping in a supermarket. One brand of soap flakes offered free towels packed with their product, and Steve bought six Large Economy Jumbo boxes of detergent, telling himself that eventually it would be all used up, that he could store the soap in the meantime in the extra bedroom, and that every penny counted.

He also bought a collection of stainless steel tableware, a half dozen plates and cups and saucers (resisting the temptation to buy even more soap of another brand, which offered free glassware in their packages) a couple of pots and pans, and enough food so that he could make his own breakfasts. The memory of the price he had paid for the bed and the chair lay heavily on his conscience.

When he returned to Forest Wood, he saw that his threat to the salesman to take his business elsewhere unless he could get immediate delivery had been heeded sooner than he had anticipated. Four huge cardboard cartons and one smaller one were in the lobby of Forest Wood, each bearing his name.

CHAPTER FIVE

STEVE WAS STANDING there looking at them help-lessly when he heard a male voice laughing behind him.

"Three'll get you five you weren't home when the friendly delivery service arrived."

He turned and saw a pleasant-faced young man with blond hair cut in the modern fashion, something that Steve, who had worn his hair short even before the Army, wasn't quite used to.

"You'd win," he said.

"I'll give you a hand if you like," the young man said. "It doesn't look like you can manage that by yourself."

"I'd appreciate it," Steve said.

"Where's it going?" the young man asked.

"Second floor, overlooking the pool," Steve said.

"Another connoisseur of the bathing beauties, I see," the young man said. "I wonder how long you'll last?"

"I beg your pardon?"

"The reason those apartments are usually available is that those who rent them (a) marry one of the beauties and (b) once they've hooked the fish, the beauties make them move."

"You sound like an expert," Steve said.

"I've been here two years," the young man said. "I guess that does make me an expert." He put out his hand. "Randy Walsh," he said.

"Steve Haas," Steve replied.

It took them twenty minutes to carry the boxes upstairs, to set up the bed, and the chair, and then to carry the cartons downstairs.

"I'd offer you a beer," Steve said. "But I didn't think to buy any."

"I'm driving at 6:30," Randy said, "and can't have one. But I'll give you one. Come on over to my place. I've got to get dressed anyway."

Steve's first impression, that Randy Walsh was a very conscientious driver who wouldn't drink a beer three hours before he was to drive, was corrected when they were in Walsh's fully furnished apartment. Walsh disappeared for a couple of minutes, and came back dressed in a blue uniform with three gold stripes on the sleeves. He was an airlines pilot, a first officer. Pilots aren't permitted any alcohol for 24 hours before they're to fly.

"When's the rest of your furniture coming?" Walsh asked, pulling open the top of a can of 7-UP.

"That's it, so far," Steve said. "I had no idea it was so expensive."

"Just move here?"

"Yeah. Transferred from Detroit. I used to live in a hotel."

"So did I," Walsh said. "But it gets pretty dull after a while. I think you'll like it here. If you need anything, speak up. I'll be gone about a week this trip. What about a television? Radio? TV tray?"

"Very good of you," Steve said. "But I'm not wild about television, and I want to buy a radio anyway. I'll borrow a TV table, though, until I can get one."

"You better take a lamp, too," Walsh said. "Unless things have changed, you're not going to find a light bulb in any socket in your apartment."

He went to a closet and took out two folding TV trays, and then went into a bedroom and returned with a gooseneck lamp.

"Here you are," he said. "Just slam the door when you leave. If you want to get back in, you'll find the key where a burglar would never think to look for it, under the rubber mat in front of the door."

"Where are you going?" Steve asked.

"London, on the first leg," Walsh said, "via New York. And then on to Rome and Istanbul. Probably wind up in Africa this trip. I'll be back in about a week or ten days. Maybe less."

Steve got up to leave.

"Sit down," Walsh said. "No need for you to go. There's nothing in your apartment anyway."

"You're a trusting soul," Steve said.

"I prefer to think of myself as an infallible judge of human character," Walsh said. "Take care of the girls while I'm gone, Steve. Don't be greedy, there's more than enough to go around."

And with that, picking up a small suitcase by the door, he was gone.

Steve thought he was a very nice guy, even if he did open his apartment to a total stranger. But he was uncomfortable in someone else's apartment, and five minutes after Walsh had gone, he picked up the TV trays and the lamp and returned to his own apartment. Walsh was right. Not one socket in the apartment, including the fluorescent fixture in the bathroom, contained a bulb.

He'd have to get some bulbs right away. But first things first. A swim was in order. He took off his clothes and laid them on the bed, and then prepared to go to the pool. Something was needed, he decided, for the proper atmosphere of nonchalance. He realized he should not look as if he was there just to look. He needed something to read.

There was, of course, no newspaper or magazine in the apartment. The only printed matter was the *Duties, Authorities and Responsibilities* manual Chennowith had given him. He picked that up, pushing the unpleasant Chennowith business from his mind, and went down to the pool. Then he went back up the stairs again, ripped open one of the huge boxes of soap flakes, and fished around inside until he found the towel. It was, as the box advertised, "Huge, a full 48 x 60 inches." It was also blushing pink. One after the other, he ripped open the other soap boxes.

Each of them contained a huge, 48 x 60-inch blushing pink towel. There was nothing he could do about it now, he realized. He wondered, as he went down the stairs, if it would be possible to dye a towel.

He swam the length of the pool twice, and then got out, preferring to let the sun dry him rather than wave the pink towel about. There were half a dozen girls at the pool, and they all looked at him, quite casually, but at the same time with obvious interest. He was pleased, of course, but he had come to the conclusion that the best way to attract girls was to appear disinterested. He reached for the manual Chennowith had given him, thumbed through it, and began to read at random.

Instantly, the passage before him really captured his attention:

23.56 DIVERGENT OPINIONS-PERSONNEL MATTERS: *Inasmuch as a potential conflict of interests between the Plant Manager, responsible to the Vice President, Fiscal, for operational costs, and the Assembly Line Manager, responsible to the Vice President, Manufacturing, for operational efficiency, may result in divergent opinions regarding staffing at both Management and Labor levels, the Assembly Line Manager, after making his position known to the Plant Manager, may appeal a personnel decision to the Vice President, Personnel, providing he presents both sides on the difference of opinion, and is convinced in his own mind that raising the question is justified in the interests of operational efficiency. In this case, the decision of the Vice President, Personnel, will be followed. Vice President, Fiscal, will be notified of the decision so that appropriate operating budget amendments may be made.*

He thought about it very carefully, almost, but not quite, to the point of shutting the girls out of his mind. No matter how often he reread it, it came out the same way: Recognizing his, the assembly line manager's, responsibilities, the company was saying that his wishes regarding the people who worked for him were important enough that he could challenge the plant manager's decisions, and have a final decision made by upper level executives.

Without ever actually having laid eyes on this man Cole, Steve had decided that Cole was entitled, since he wasn't going to get the promotion he'd been told he'd been given, at least to the raise he was told he had. Not only was that simple fairness, but not giving it to him was going to hurt his morale. If his morale was affected, so would his efficiency be affected. That was liable to cost the company more money than the raise represented.

Something else came into Steve's mind, too. Certainly Pickens, as plant manager, was, or should be, aware of this company policy. Yet he had bluntly told Steve on the telephone that it was his decision, and implied that there was nothing Steve could do about it, once he'd made up his mind. The unpleasant conclusion to draw from that was that Pickens either didn't know his job, or did know it, and had lied to Steve.

Steve resolved to see Pickens first thing in the morning.

He did see him first thing in the morning, too, the very first thing. As he drove past the shopping center which served Forest Wood and the subdivisions surrounding it, his eye caught a sign advertising a sale on light bulbs. He pulled in, and bought a case of bulbs.

When he got to the plant, he carried the case inside with him. He was going to have the rental car company pick up the car at the plant, and it seemed the logical thing to carry the bulbs into his office now.

He met Pickens in the lobby.

"Good morning, sir," Steve said.

"Haas," Pickens said. "What's that? Light bulbs?"

"Yes, sir," Steve said.

"May I ask what you're going to do with a case of light bulbs?"

I'm going to stick them in my ears so they light up when I stick my tongue out, Steve thought, but he had enough sense to answer, "They were on sale, sir, and I bought them."

"I see," Pickens said, his tone suggesting that carrying a case of light bulbs was somehow beneath the dignity of an Amalgamated executive.

"If you have time, sir," Steve said. "I'd like to have a word with you as soon as I can."

"By all means, Haas," Pickens said. "Drop off your light bulbs and come right in."

"Thank you, sir," Steve said.

He stopped in his own office just long enough to tell Miss Fallon to have the rental car picked up, and to give her the keys and his credit card to pay for it, and then he went down to Pickens' office.

He was annoyed, but somehow not surprised when after having been told to come right down, Pickens kept him waiting for ten minutes before allowing him in his office.

"Sorry to have kept you waiting, Steve," he said. "What can I do for you?"

"I'd like to talk about Mr. Cole," Steve said.

"What about him?"

"I'd like to see that he gets to keep the pay raise he was told he was going to get, and I would like to name him night manager," Steve said. "Or maybe I should say that the other way around; I'd like to name him night manager and in that way see that he gets the pay raise he was promised."

"Your memory's not very good, is it?" Pickens said. "We reached a decision on this yesterday."

"You reached a decision," Steve said. "I'm here to ask you to reconsider."

"Mr. Haas, why don't you wait until you have just a little experience around here before you start making requests that I change my mind?"

"The company started paying me yesterday, Mr. Pickens, to start making decisions."

"Well, then, I'll spell it out for you one final time, since that seems necessary. I decline either to name Mr. Cole night manager, or to raise his pay, because his pay raise was based on his assumption of duties which he did not assume. The company, in its wisdom, has seen fit to assign you to us, and you know how that has progressively bumped people down the line."

"Mr. Pickens," Steve said. "I've been reading the *Duties, Authorities and Responsibilities* manual."

"I'm sure you'll find it quite helpful, since by your own admission, you know very little about your new duties."

"The manual offers a— The manual permits me to appeal a decision of this nature," Steve said.

"I beg your pardon?" Pickens said coldly.

"I said, the manual gives the assembly line manager the right to appeal personnel decisions of this type."

"I see," Pickens said. "And you actually— Mr. Haas, you do whatever you think is best in your interest and the company's, of course."

"Yes, sir," Steve said. "Thank you for seeing me, Mr. Pickens."

"If your schedule will permit, Mr. Haas," Pickens said, "could you arrange to have luncheon with us at half past twelve in the canteen? I'd like to introduce you to the rest of the management team."

"Yes, sir," Steve said. "Thank you, I'll be there."

When he walked back to his own office, he found a man about fifty in the office. Bald, ruddy faced, he looked the kind of man who would have worked his way up in the company from a spot on the assembly line.

"Are you Mr. Cole?" Steve asked.

"That's right."

"I'm Steve Haas," Steve said. "I'd like very much to talk to you, but I've got to make a telephone call first. Have you got time to wait a couple of minutes?"

"You're the boss," Cole said. "I'm at your disposal."

"Get Mr. Cole some coffee, will you please, Miss

Fallon?" Steve said. "And then get me Mr. Tornell, please."

"Mr. Tornell?" she asked.

"In Personnel, in Detroit," Steve said.

"Yes, sir," she said.

He went into his office and closed the door. He was not unaware that he was picking a fight with the boss even before he'd seen the inside of the plant. But it was the sort of thing he didn't think he could put off. It was an unpleasant situation no matter how you looked at it, but there was no retreating. He had to go on.

"Mr. Chennowith is here, Mr. Haas," the intercom said.

"Ask him to—wait with Mr. Cole, please," Steve said. "When I'm off the phone, ask them to come in."

"I have Mr. Tornell on the line," she said.

He reached for the telephone. It had a row of buttons, two of which were lit up. He pushed one of them, and Miss Fallon came on the line. "Yes, Mr. Haas?"

"I'll take Mr. Tornell now," he said.

"Push the other button," she said, and she sounded rather close to a giggle.

He pushed the other button.

"Mr. Tornell?" he asked.

"One moment, please," a feminine voice in Detroit said. "Mr. Haas is on the line, Mr. Tornell."

Then Tornell's voice: "Well, how are things in Alabama, Mr. Haas?"

"I seem to have stirred up sort of a mess down here," Steve said.

"Yes, I've heard," Tornell said. "Anything I can do?"

"Well, before they knew I was coming, they appointed a man named Cole to fill the vacancy of

Chennowith, who was supposed to take the assembly line."

"Yes, so I understand."

"I would like to see that Mr. Cole is appointed night manager of the assembly line, and given the same category and pay advance he would have received if I hadn't shown up."

"I think I see what you mean," Tornell said. "But why are you calling me? Isn't that a decision for Mr. Pickens?"

"I've brought the matter up to Mr. Pickens, and he doesn't agree," Steve said.

"Then why bother, Mr. Haas, to call me? Doesn't that settle the matter?"

"Not according to the Manual. The Manual says I can appeal the decision."

"What manual?"

"Duties, Authorities and Responsibilities," Steve said.

"Haas," Tornell said, almost gently. "Let me give you a word of advice. While those manuals are highly desirable for lower level management positions, one seldom pays much attention to them at your level, for the very good reason that yours is the level at which you're paid to make decisions, not to follow the book."

It was a reprimand; worse, it was being tolerated.

"Well, the Manual says I can appeal the decision, and I'm appealing it right now."

"Does Mr. Pickens know you're telephoning me?"

"More or less," Steve said. "I told him I was going to appeal the decision, and he told me that I should do what I thought best in my interest and the company's."

"I see," Tornell said. "Then this is an official action?"

"I guess you could call it that," Steve said.

"Very well," Tornell said. "I'll have to presume you know what you're doing. I'll be in touch with you shortly."

"How shortly?" Steve asked, and even as he asked, he knew he shouldn't have.

Tornell was cold when he replied, "Just as soon, Mr. Haas, as I can fit it into my schedule. You're one of twenty-two assembly line managers, you know. There are others in the company who also have problems."

"Thank you," Steve said. "Good-bye, Mr. Tornell." He hung up. He looked out the window. In a moment, he heard the door squeak slightly as it opened. He turned to face Chennowith.

"Good morning, Steve," Chennowith said. "Can I come in?"

"Sure, and ask Mr. Cole to come in, too," Steve said. He pushed the button on his intercom: "Miss Fallon, would you bring me some coffee, too?"

When the coffee had been delivered, and Miss Fallon had gone, Chennowith said, "Steve, I did something last night maybe I shouldn't have done."

"What's that?"

"Howard and I are old friends," Chennowith said. "I called him and told him what had happened. Maybe I shouldn't have. But I thought it would be easier all around that way."

"No harm done, anyway," Steve said. "I was just on the horn to Detroit."

"Pardon me?" Chennowith said.

"I want to have you named, Mr. Cole, as night assembly line manager."

"I thought Mr. Pickens turned down that idea," Chennowith said.

"He did," Steve said. "I'm appealing the decision."

"You went over Pickens' head?" Cole said. It was the first thing he'd said.

"Not the way it sounds," Steve said. "That manual you loaned me, Bob, gives me that right."

"He's not going to like that," Chennowith said.

"And you can't really blame him," Cole said.

"Whose side are you on, Mr. Cole?" Steve said.

"I've been with the company twenty-two years, Mr. Haas," Cole said. "I long ago learned to roll with the punches. You didn't really have to fight my battle for me."

Steve felt anger swell up inside him. It took him almost a minute before he trusted himself to speak.

"Would you care to clarify that, Mr. Cole?" he asked finally.

"The company would have taken care of me," Cole said blandly. "I've got some friends in high places, too. I wasn't going to take this lying down."

"I don't think I like that crack about friends in high places," Steve said.

"I started out in the business on the assembly line, Mr. Haas," Cole said. "Putting brake shoes on drums. I know my way around."

"I started out in this business replacing worn-out brake shoes in a garage," Steve said. "But I don't see what that's got to do with this."

"What Mr. Cole means, Steve—"

"What I mean is that if I don't like what's going on around here, I can put in for retirement," Cole said. "I don't need someone with three years with the company taking care of me."

Chennowith actually winced.

"Let me tell you something, Cole," Steve said. "I'm not taking care of you. I'm doing what I think is in the company's best interests. And as no one asked me if I wanted this job, I'm not asking you if you want the job as night manager. You either take it, or put in for retirement."

"Providing you don't get slapped down into your proper place by Detroit," Cole said.

Steve waited another full minute before he opened his mouth again. "Thank you for coming in, Mr. Cole," he said. "You may return to your duties. When I need you again, I'll send for you."

When Cole had gone, Steve looked at Chennowith, who then said: "I'm sorry about that, Steve. I apparently didn't do a very good job of spreading oil on the waters last night."

"I guess they were pretty rough waters," Steve said.

"I'm torn between two loyalties," Chennowith said. "But I think you're entitled to know that Pickens got to Cole before I did. By the time I got him on the phone, he was already boiling. And he's not kidding about having friends in high places, either. You can't help but have, if you do a good job for the company as long as he has."

Steve, without thinking, said something cruel. "If he's done such a good job, how come he's not sitting here, or in Pickens' office? Do you suppose it might be because he hasn't learned to keep his mouth shut?"

Chennowith seemed startled, and then he laughed. "I get the feeling that you're not quite as vulnerable as everybody seems to think."

"Is that what everybody thinks?" Steve replied, annoyed, and then: "Well, aren't we supposed to have a car made for me today?"

CHAPTER SIX

STEVE DID FEEL vulnerable, in the sense that he didn't really understand half of what Chennowith tried to explain to him about the assembly of his car. The explanation began with a computer card in the office.

Each car to come off the line was assembled according to the holes punched in the small piece of stiff paper. A hole in a certain position indicated the body style, whether two-door, or hardtop, or four-door or convertible or station wagon. Another hole indicated the color, or colors, and another the type and color of upholstery. Still other holes indicated the size of tires, and whether black or whitewall.

The card had a number of functions. In addition to listing all the components (a phrase meaning two or more parts assembled together and received at East

Point as a unit, such as carburetors) and parts (a "part" was just one part, whether a tire, or a headlight, or a screw to hold down the aluminum kickplate in the door well), the card was used to see that the parts and components arrived at the proper spot on the line at the proper time, to be installed in, or attached to, the right car.

The term assembly line wasn't really very accurate. There were three lines at East Point down which parts moved, were joined together and emerged at the end as running automobiles.

One line was entirely devoted to the most popular Mohawk, the four-door Crescent. There were three models of the Crescent, starting with the Crescent Mark II (there was no Mark I) which was the stripped-down version, with a three-speed stick shift and a 6-cylinder engine and plain upholstery. The Crescent Mark III had a V-8 engine, an automatic transmission, and somewhat fancier upholstery. The top of the line was the Crescent 950, which had a larger V-8 engine, a different automatic transmission, and even fancier upholstery, to include a vinyl covering on the roof.

The second assembly line assembled two-door sedans, hardtops and convertibles, and the third put together station wagons (three different models) and pick-up trucks (five different models).

To either side of the main assembly lines in the plant were sub-assembly lines, feeding their products to the main assembly lines. Two of these, for example, were devoted to engines, one for six-cylinder engines and one for V-8 engines. There were four different six-cylinder engines, and three different V-8 engines. The engines arrived by rail from the engine assembly plant in Hamtranck, Michigan, lacking most of their accessories. They had fuel pumps, but no carburetors, because the computer card would determine which engine got the two-barrel carburetor, for example, instead of the four-barrel. They had no fans, because the computer card would determine which engine was to get the standard fan, and which was to get the larger fan belt, mounted on an extension, because the car in which it would be installed would have an air conditioner, and would require the extra cooling and extension.

Wheels, which came in three different sizes, arrived from that many different manufacturing plants, one owned by Amalgamated, and the others independent businesses. The wheels were painted only with a priming coat. They were painted, as were all other body components, at East Point, because that was the only way they could be sure that the fenders and hoods and wheels would have exactly the same hue of yellow or blue.

Once painted, the wheels were fitted with tires, balanced, and fed into the line.

Only a very few components could be said to fit every car, fewer than Steve had at first thought. There were even three different colors for the handle on cigarette lighters, white, black and chrome.

Steve formed a mental picture of a metal kitchen funnel into which parts were apparently dumped at random, and from which, miraculously, cars poured out the small end. It was obvious that he had a great deal to learn about his new job; his awareness of his ignorance gave him good reason to doubt his "brave" stand in standing up to Pickens.

"From the time we put this card into the system, Steve, it takes about twenty minutes for the first component, the frame, to appear on the assembly line," Chennowith said.

"What happens to the card after the car is made?" Steve asked.

"It's by no means finished," Chennowith said.

"The first thing that happens to it is that it's returned to the computer for parts re-order. We maintain a supply of parts ranging from a couple of shifts' supply to maybe two weeks. Generally, the smaller the part, the more we have on hand, although that's not hard and fast. Sometimes, the on-hand supply depends in large measure on how many fit on a boxcar. Fenders, for example, body panels, that sort of thing. Upholstery material comes in large quantities on one car, if you consider the material. When you think of what goes under the material, above the spring, one carload doesn't last long."

"Where do you get the springs?" Steve asked. "For the seats, I mean?"

"We make them here, either bent wire for the cheaper models, or coiled wire, coiled springs, for the Warriors."

"Coil wheel springs and leaf springs are shipped in?"

"Both are shipped in," Chennowith said. "Heavy springs require a heat-treating process that really doesn't belong in an assembly plant."

"Let's put the card into the works," Steve said, "and see what happens."

As they went to the assembly building itself, Steve asked another question, fully aware that it revealed still more of his magnificent ignorance.

"What about the cars that are just shipped to dealers?" Steve asked. "Do they order every car individually on one of these computer cards?"

"No. That's where the card comes into use again. A dealer's stock order, that is, when he tells the Region to ship him so many cars, without specifying precisely what he wants, is generally made up by marketing. They get the output of the computer, too. They know, within decimal points, how many cars should have radios, for example, about ninety per cent, and that so many per cent should have white wall tires, or air conditioners, or should be of such and such a model. Based on what the dealers sell, they constantly change their figures."

"But the dealer can order any car he wants?"

"Like your card, which is being handled like a dealer special order, it takes twenty minutes from the time we put it into the system, until the first component appears on the main assembly line. But what they've found out, although we're perfectly happy to make up a car any way it's wanted, is that the customer nine times out of ten will see something on the showroom floor that he wants, right then, and buys it right then, rather than waiting what amounts to maybe a week from the time he places the order until we can deliver the car to the dealer."

"I don't know anything about sales, either," Steve said. "I'm beginning to feel like the dummy of all time."

"The line isn't as complicated as it sounds at first," Chennowith said. "There are all kinds of stops built into it. The line will stop, for example, if the wrong component is fed into it. If we send four doors to a two-door frame, the line stops, and the expediters try to straighten it out as quickly as they can, shunting the parts where they properly belong, seeing that the proper parts go back on the line. If the line stops, and the line has, say, as ours do, about three hundred men on it at a time, each making about five dollars an hour, all told, including fringe benefits, that means that a shut-down line is costing the company $1500 an hour, or $25 a minute."

"I didn't realize that there were that many men on a line," Steve said.

"More or less, depending on how you count them, whether the final assembly, or the semi-final assembly, or the primary assembly; whether you include the painters, or the upholsterers, the inspectors, or the guys who drive the cars away. Twenty-five dollars a minute is conservative, I suppose."

They entered an office, and Chennowith took the computer card and handed it to a clerk.

"We're going to walk through with it," he said.

"Take about eighteen minutes, the way the line is going now," the clerk said. "We're heavy on air conditioners today, that slows it down some."

Chennowith pushed open an interior door and waved Steve through. The noise was deafening. They walked up along the line, slowly, to a point where machinery brought in frames. The mechanic, rather than the engineer, in Steve was fascinated. The whole thing was a mechanical marvel. Clamps picked up a frame from a stack of them, stacked vertically, and moved them to the start of the line. At once, workmen began to install other parts and components, the front suspension first, and fifteen feet away, the rear suspension and rear axle. Just a few feet farther along, another conveyor lowered an engine assembly in position, and workmen bolted it in place.

While he was glad that Chennowith had suggested he "walk through" with his car as it was assembled, it was immediately apparent to Steve that walking through wouldn't really teach him very much at all. He would have to spend a long time on the line, a long time at each station, before he understood how any of it really worked.

He was down on his knees, watching how frame assemblies were supported by metal fixtures which came out of the floor just in time to take the frame from the clamps carrying it to the line, when he became aware that his name was being called. It had to be shouted to be heard over the din. Steve stood up, and saw that Chennowith was talking to a man in work clothes. The man looked somehow familiar, and he seemed to look at Steve with recognition.

Even cupping his hand to his ear, Steve couldn't hear what was being said, so Chennowith took both of them by the arm and pushed them into the glass-walled administrative work space which paralleled the line.

"Steve," Chennowith said, when the door closed out most, but by no means all, of the noise. "This is Terry Fallon. He's the union steward, and part of our contract with the union says that we can't have visitors to the assembly line as a safety measure. They distract the workmen. I was just explaining."

"I know this ugly Irishman," Steve said.

"So it is you," Fallon said. "All dressed up in a tie and suit, just like you were human."

"I didn't recognize you with a shave and a bath," Steve said. "Who held you down?"

"Somebody a lot stronger than you, you miserable grease monkey," Fallon said, and then to Chennowith's visible shock, the two embraced each other, and pounded each other soundly on the back and punched each other on the arms, beaming broadly.

"I gather you know each other," Chennowith said drily.

"I gave him his first bath," Steve said.

"We were in the Army together," Fallon explained. "Steve was my motor sergeant."

"I see," Chennowith said.

"I heard your name," Fallon said. "Janet came home and screamed loudly about the shake Chennowith got from some guy named Haas. I didn't figure there was much chance it was you, though, even with that weird name."

"What do you do here?"

"I'm foreman of frame and power plant final assembly," Fallon said. "And shop steward for the union. I was just about to have you tossed out."

"You're related to the redhead?" Steve asked.

"My sister," Fallon said. "She's not one of your admirers, Steve. She spent most of last night sticking pins in a doll with a sign on him with your name."

"I had that feeling," Steve said.

Fallon asked the question that came to his mind. "How did you ever wind up with a job like this?"

"That seems to be the question of the day," Steve said.

Fallon looked up at the wall, above the glass opening on the assembly line. A rear-lighted board was mounted there, bearing numbers. The number showed the car about to be assembled.

"That's the one you're waiting for, Steve," Fallon said, gesturing toward it. "You want to walk through with it, you better go. See you later?"

"I'll buy you a beer after work," Steve said. "Where can I find you?"

"I generally stop by at the VFW on the main street outside for a beer. I knock off at 4:30. See you?"

"I'll be there," Steve said. Fallon opened the door, and the sound drowned out any further chance to talk.

The way the car was assembled was astonishing. It moved down the assembly line at the pace of a brisk walk, and seemed to take shape like trick photography. One moment, the engine was exposed, and the next, metallic fingers were holding fenders in place, while the workmen bolted them on. By the time Steve decided to take a look into the engine compartment, to see how the bolting was actually accomplished, the conveyor was lowering the hood assembly in place, and workmen were bolting the tension springs to the cowling.

The only time he really had a chance to look at the

car for more than a couple of seconds at a time was during final inspection, after it was assembled and fuel had been put into the gas tank and water into the radiator. An inspector in a smock got in, and made a final check of all the accessories, running the windows and the top up and down, turning the radio on and off, operating the air conditioner and the heater, sliding the seat back and forth, even blowing the horn.

Then he got out of the car and handed the inspection sheet to Chennowith.

"Looks all right to me, Mr. Chennowith," he said. "Any special reason you wanted to walk through with this one?"

"It's Mr. Haas's car," Chennowith said. "Mr. Haas is the new assembly line manager."

The inspector, an intelligent-looking man in his mid-forties, who probably had worked his way up from the line looked at Steve with curiosity, but there was no welcome or warmth in his eyes.

"How do you do?" Steve said.

"How are you?" the inspector said. "Does this car go into stock, or what?"

"Find a place to put it until we can get Mr. Haas some license plates for it," Chennowith said. "We can send Janet for them, I suppose."

Steve looked at his watch. It was a few minutes after ten.

"What normally happens around this time of morning?" Steve asked.

"Well, I normally hold management conferences, starting at nine-thirty," Chennowith said. "The division and department and branch chiefs. Cole's running them this morning. Would you like to go?"

"I think I'd better," Steve said.

The conference was held in a large, barren room holding four library tables pushed together. Aside from the tables, the chairs, and a blackboard, the room held no other furnishings except a telephone and a row of photographs of Mohawk automobiles on its concrete block walls.

Steve and Chennowith took seats at the table. Cole neither introduced Steve, nor acknowledged Chennowith's presence. Steve learned a great deal from the conference, in addition to confirming his belief that his lack of knowledge was staggering.

Each of the assembly lines was termed a division, with a division chief. There were a number of departments, each charged with a specific responsibility to all of the lines, such as the painting and upholstery, engine and power train departments. Some of the larger departments, each of which had a department manager, had branches, under a branch supervisor. Engines, for example, were broken down into two departments, each under a supervisor, one for six-cylinder engines and the other for V-8's. Similarly, there was a branch and a branch supervisor for automatic and standard transmissions.

At the conferences, which were held at least twice a day, each man with a specific responsibility brought up his problems. Problems were anything that happened to keep the line from moving smoothly. This could be a shortage of workers, a shortage of parts, such as an unusually heavy demand for one kind of engine over another, which would make it necessary to have increased supplies of that particular kind of engine shipped in ahead of a prearranged schedule, or anything of that nature.

The problems were gathered together, and then passed on to other departments of the assembly plant itself for resolution or assistance. A shortage of workers would be the ultimate responsibility of the personnel manager, who would have to arrange with the union hall for more men to replace absentees, or to handle additional work. The director of administration, the Number Two man at the plant, whom Steve had yet to meet, was informed of unusual demands for parts and components manufactured within Amalgamated Motors.

If the system started to break down, Steve saw, everybody got involved. If there was a demand, for example, for an unusual number of Mohawk Warrior 450 engines, the largest engine, beyond the "programmed" requirements (which meant, Steve understood, a studied guess), the director of administration would order the engines from the engine assembly plant. The director of purchasing would see that the carburetors (not made by AMC) were ordered for delivery on time. The transportation manager would make sure that the engines and the carburetors would either arrive at the plant on time aboard already scheduled railroad boxcars, or contract trucks, or he would make arrangements for special truck or rail transportation.

The responsibility of the assembly line manager ended with making his requirements known to the Upper Management conference. They were responsible for providing him with the parts and components and the people to make the cars. He was responsible for putting the cars together, and his responsibility for the cars ended when they were driven through the gate in the hurricane fence, and became the responsibility of the transportation manager.

Everyone in the room, with one exception, was wearing a shirt and tie. Some wore smocks over their shirts, others regular jackets. The exception, a man in his thirties, was wearing work clothes, and a hard hat sat before him on the table.

In front of each chair at the table was a pad of lined paper and several pencils. Steve leaned forward and wrote on the pad, "Who's the guy in the hard hat?" and slid it over to Chennowith.

Chennowith wrote: "Tony Cassilio, Chief of Line Equipment Branch."

Steve nodded. He could figure that out himself. Cassilio was the man responsible for keeping the line physically going, responsible for the conveyors and the power tools. Steve indulged in a bit of wishful thinking. That was the job he really would have liked to have. That looked fascinating. He envied Cassilio.

Then the incredible thought occurred to him that he was the boss of everybody in this room, Cassilio included. He thought that Janet Fallon had every right in the world to think that Chennowith had been treated unfairly. It made no sense at all to put a man in charge of an operation like this who knew nothing whatever about it.

He was brought from his thoughts by Cole's voice.

"That'll do for now. Unless you've got something, Mr. Chennowith?"

"Just one small, minor, unimportant thing, Howard," Chennowith said, getting up. "I think everybody would like to meet the new boss. Gentlemen, this is Mr. Haas, who has been named assembly line manager."

There were very few smiles of welcome, but everybody looked at Steve. In the time it took him to stand up, Steve considered making the open confession that he felt that he was in five or six feet over his head in his new job. He decided against it. That word probably was already out. What he would have to do would be to learn his job, but for the time being to act as if he was perfectly sure of his own ability to fill it.

"I'm glad Mr. Chennowith saw fit to introduce me," he said. "I intend to spend as much time as possible in the immediate future taking a good close look at the line. And already this morning, one of the foremen tried to give me the heave-ho."

There was, as he expected there would be, some laughter at this.

"Until I get my feet on the ground," Steve said, "Mr. Chennowith will continue to be the man where the buck stops. I'm glad to be here, and that's about all I've got to say."

He sat down.

"That's it, fellas," Cole said. "Next meeting's at three."

Chennowith leaned over and whispered, "Go stand by the door and shake hands."

Steve got up, and one by one, Chennowith introduced the men as they filed out. Only Cassilio had something to say besides "How do you do?"

"Weren't you involved with the Hawke Model 19, Mr. Haas?"

"Yes, I was," Steve said.

"I thought I recognized your name and face," Cassilio said. "Glad to have you with us."

"Thank you," Steve said.

When they had all gone, Chennowith asked, "What's the Hawke Model 19? Or shouldn't I ask?"

"Racing car," Steve said. "Designed and built by an Englishman. The AMC plant in Giessen, Germany, tried to build up a transmission for it. I got involved."

"As the design engineer?"

"Not really," Steve said. "I was more or less an errand boy there, too. I served as liaison between Hawke and Amalgamated Giessen G.m.b.H., and AMC Engineering."

"Whatever happened to the car?"

"It was a financial disaster," Steve said truthfully. "We did the best we could, but it just didn't come off."

"Well, we'd better hurry," Chennowith said. "The upper management conference is supposed to start at eleven. It's already five after. We're always late for it."

CHAPTER SEVEN

JANET FALLON WAS standing outside Pickens' office when Steve and Chennowith entered the building for the upper management conference.

"This came for you, Mr. Haas," she said, and handed him a folded-over Telex message.

FROM VICE PRESIDENT, PERSONNEL DETROIT
TO GENERAL MANAGER, ASSEMBLY PLANT 15 EAST
POINT GA

INFO COPY TO ASSEMBLY LINE MANAGER PLANT 15
HOWARD G. COLE WILL BE APPOINTED TO THE
NEWLY CREATED POSITION OF NIGHT ASSEMBLY
LINE MANAGER AT CATEGORY 24, BY DIRECTION OF
VICE PRESIDENT, PERSONNEL, WITH CONCURRENCE

VICE PRESIDENT, ADMINISTRATION. VICE PRESI-
DENT, FISCAL, HAS BEEN NOTIFIED.

JEROME B. TORNELL

"Thank you, Janet," Steve said. He handed the
Telex to Chennowith.

"You won," Chennowith said. "But you may wish
you hadn't."

"It was only fair," Steve said.

"Janet," Chennowith said, "while we're in here,
how about registering Mr. Haas's car?" He handed
her a thin stack of papers, and Steve took money
from his pocket and gave it to her.

"Oh, is your car ready, Mr. Haas?" she said, and she
smiled. She was obviously trying to make peace, most
likely because of the battle he'd fought and won on
behalf of Cole. Possibly because he was still a little
angry about Cole's attitude, and possibly because he
had an odd sense of humor, he replied:

"Well, it's ready,but I have very serious doubts
about it."

"How's that?" she asked, genuinely concerned.

"Well, if the frame and power plant assembly foreman is typical of the work force, I'll be surprised if it
makes it downtown without falling apart," Steve
said. "I don't think I have ever seen an uglier workman, either, come to think of it."

Janet Fallon went absolutely white in the face, and
then turned on her heel and marched down the corridor. For the first time since he'd arrived at the
plant, Steve felt just slightly pleased with himself.

Chennowith pushed the door open for him, and
Steve walked into Pickens' office. As soon as he saw
the look on Pickens' face, he knew that Pickens had
received his copy of the Telex message, and the good

feeling vanished without trace, as if it had never been there.

"We schedule these meetings, Mr. Haas," Pickens said, "for eleven. I would appreciate it very much if you would make an attempt to adhere to that schedule."

"Yes, sir," Steve said. "I'll do my best."

"Gentlemen," Pickens said, as Steve walked into his office. "This is Mr. Haas, who has come to us from a position as a supervisory engineer in the office of Mr. Stuart Whitman in Detroit." He paused. "I'm sure we all hope that Mr. Whitman's faith in his ability to operate our assembly line will be justified."

One by one, Steve was introduced to the assistant plant manager, a gray-haired man in his fifties; to the director of purchasing, the youngest, at about 45, of all of them; the director of administration, and the transportation manager.

"With your permission, sir," Steve said, "Mr. Chennowith will represent me at these meetings until I get my feet on the ground."

"Whatever you think best, of course, Mr. Haas," Pickens said. "But I must confess that I'm rather disappointed. I had rather looked forward to the benefit of your thinking."

There was nothing Steve could reply to that, so he said nothing. He hoped that it was only a sensation, and that his neck wasn't really getting red.

Pickens had very carefully made it plain what he thought of Steve—had, in a manner of speaking, declared war on him. And there was absolutely nothing he could do about it, Steve realized, except hope that he could learn his job before Pickens could manage to take it away from him. That he would try to do just that was obvious.

"I have only one thing to say, gentlemen," Steve said, aware that he couldn't just sit there like a frightened rabbit. "At my request, Detroit has given me an additional personnel space in upper management. I have named Mr. Howard Cole as night assembly line manager. That makes him the Number Three man in my division, and I ask you to make this known to whoever needs to know it."

"Thank you, Mr. Haas," Pickens said coldly. "I had planned to make that announcement. Mr. Haas felt so strongly, on the basis of his first day in his new assignment, that he chose to appeal my decision on the matter to Detroit. Detroit upheld him. They apparently have a high regard for him."

Steve knew that his neck was red. He looked down at his hands. They were balled in tight fists, and the knuckles were white. With an effort, he unclenched them, and with a greater effort, he put a smile on his face.

"I understand I've delayed the opening of the meeting," he said. "Can we begin?"

The meeting lasted until twelve-twenty-five. Steve thought he was beginning to form a vague idea of how things worked, although, as the meeting progressed, he was convinced that Pickens had made no effort to explain anything to him. Since Pickens was making no effort to explain anything, the others took their cue from him, and went on as if Steve weren't present in the room.

When Pickens adjourned the meeting, they walked in a group to the plant canteen, a cafeteria operation with two smaller dining rooms opening off the main room.

There were no signs, but Steve saw that they would have been unnecessary. The largest room, where people stood in line carrying trays, was for the workmen. The next smaller was for foremen, and the food was served by waitresses. The smallest room was for "management," and Steve formed another quick opinion which he realized was none of his business. He thought that if management was going to eat in the canteen, they should stand in the cafeteria line like anyone else.

If the plant were his, and he thought there was a need for a special dining room with special treatment for the brass, he would have put it some place where the workmen couldn't see it. Despite the welcoming smile of the mess sergeant, colonels and generals had never really been welcome in the enlisted men's mess hall, and the brass here were just as unwelcome.

And so, Steve decided, was S. Haas, assembly line manager, unwelcome at the upper management table here. It wasn't that the others were hostile to him, but rather that he represented trouble where there had been peace. The boss didn't like him, that was obvious. But on the other hand, someone in the company, at a level higher than themselves, did like him. The only way to treat Haas, it had obviously been decided, was with absolute neutrality, perhaps in the hope that if they didn't notice him, he might go away.

Before that lunch was over, Steve vowed that he would never eat at the table again, unless he was specifically ordered to.

The afternoon went much more quickly than he had thought it would go. After spending an hour reading the papers which Miss Fallon had put in his basket, trying without success to make sense out of them before turning them over to Chennowith, he sent for Cole.

"I don't know whether the word has been passed to you or not, Mr. Cole," Steve said. "But I have been given ·authority to appoint you as night assembly manager."

"I heard the rumor," Cole said. "But Chennowith

didn't say anything to me, if that's what you're asking."

"I thought perhaps you might have heard directly from Mr. Pickens," Steve said.

"As a matter of fact, I did," Cole said.

"And what did you tell him—that you would take the job or not?"

Cole seemed slightly hesitant, then: "Well, since you went to all that trouble, I figured I'd better wait until I heard from you before saying anything."

"Well, are you going to take it or not?"

"I expect maybe I owe that much to the company," Cole said. "It wouldn't be right for me to retire just when the company needs me."

"I'm glad you feel that way," Steve said.

"Have I got any instructions?" Cole said.

"I'm not sure," Steve said, "that I have the nerve to give you any orders." He paused. "You run it the way you think it should be run. If you need any help, which seems unlikely, see Mr. Chennowith."

"Chennowith tells me I was way out of line this morning, Mr. Haas. If I was, I apologize."

"None's required," Steve said. "Do you think you could bring yourself to call me 'Steve'?"

"All right, if that's the way you want it."

"Thank you, Mr. Cole," Steve said. "If it's all the same to you, I'll just keep right on calling you Mr. Cole."

"Suit yourself," Cole said, but he smiled. "You're the boss."

Soon after he was through with Cole, it was time for the afternoon meeting with the assembly line management people. That lasted until 4:35. Forty minutes remained in the established "administrative work day." Office personnel and some others worked an eight-hour shift starting and ending 45 minutes later than the work force for the assembly line. The reasoning was that by staggering the shifts, there would be less of a traffic jam at the plant gates.

Terry Fallon had said he would meet Steve at the VFW immediately after his shift was over at 4:30. Steve debated calling Pickens and telling him he was leaving and then decided against it. He was supposed to be an executive, and that carried with it the clear implication that he was supposed to make decisions. If he couldn't decide for himself when he could leave the plant, he obviously wouldn't be much of an executive. In his office, when he picked up the keys and registration to the new car from Janet Fallon, Chennowith was there. As much to annoy her as anything else, he told Chennowith, "I've had enough of this place for one day; I'm going to go get a beer."

Janet Fallon flashed him the look of disapproval he expected. He didn't think this was the time to tell her that he was going to drink that beer with her brother. He picked up the case of light bulbs he'd carried into the plant that morning and walked down the corridor, down the stairs, and out of the building.

The car smelled new; there is a special smell in a new car, and Steve liked the smell, even though by now he should be used to it. About the only people who got inside more new cars than he did were the drive-away men at the end of the assembly line.

Before moving out of his parking place, he lowered the roof. As he drove to the gate, he thought idly, when he was sixteen, seventeen, even when he'd been in college, he'd really been hungry for a car like this, had dreamed of owning one. Now that the reality was here, most of the thrill was gone. His only real reaction to the car was one of annoyance. One of the assemblers, somewhere, hadn't done his job right. The knob on the radio came off in his hand when he tried to turn the radio on.

The VFW where he was to meet Terry wasn't hard

to find. It sat off the highway, in the middle of a parking lot, and it seemed to be the first place the work force headed for when the shift was over.

He pushed the doorbell, and then had to fumble in his wallet for his VFW card before they'd let him in. He saw, too, the not entirely friendly glance he was getting from the bartender-doorkeeper. He was just a little too dressed up.

"I'm looking for Terry Fallon" he said, after he'd shown the membership card certifying his right to come in.

"Down the bar, halfway," the bartender said, and he seemed to grow just slightly more friendly.

Steve stepped behind Terry and jabbed him in the rib cage with each of his index fingers. Terry jumped and yelped, and the men on either side of him looked at Steve in surprise.

"You know I hate that," Terry said.

"Yeah, I remember," Steve said.

"Am I supposed to call you 'sir' now, or what?" Terry asked.

"Not unless you learned how to fight better than you could the last time I saw you," Steve said.

"Give this ugly chair-warmer a beer," Terry said to the bartender. Then he jerked his thumb at Steve and said, "This is Steve Haas. Proving that the Army never knows what it's doing, he was my sergeant in the Army."

After the introductions were made, one of the men with Terry asked, "Didn't I see you on the line with the boss, Steve? With Chennowith?"

"What you saw, Harry," Terry Fallon said, "was Chennowith on the line, with his boss."

"No fooling? That story's true, is it?"

"There's just as much of a grapevine here, Steve," Terry said, "as we ever had in the Army."

"I need some help, Terry," Steve said.

"Name it, buddy," Terry replied.

"I can write what I know about an assembly line with a grease pencil on a matchbook," Steve said.

"How come you got the job?"

"I expect the real reason, Terry, was like the kid being thrown in the creek to see if that won't teach him how to swim."

"What were you doing before?"

"I was on the tire and suspension test track in Texas when they called me back to Detroit and told me I was getting this job."

"You went to college when you got out, didn't you?" Terry asked.

"Yeah."

"Finish?"

"Yeah."

"Good for you," Terry said. "What's the problem with the line, then? It's not that complicated."

"Changing brakes on a truck is complicated if you never did it before," Steve said.

"We got pretty good at that after a while, though, didn't we?" Terry said, laughing.

"Let's hope so," Steve said.

"How can I help you?" Terry asked.

"Show me how it works, from one end to the other," Steve said.

"Sure," Terry said. "Be glad to. Just let me know when."

"Now," Steve said. "You have big plans for the evening?"

"That's how he got to be a sergeant," Terry said to the others. "None of this business about waiting until tomorrow." He punched Steve on the arm. "No plans at all. What do you say we grab a hamburger here— best in Atlanta, they say—and then go back out? We can't do it all in one night, but we can spend a couple of hours out there, and then have a couple of beers, too."

"I'd appreciate it, buddy," Steve said.

"I'll let you buy the hamburgers," Terry said.

"You're on," Steve said.

"What did you study in college?" Terry asked.

"The diploma says I'm an automotive engineer," Steve replied.

"You want to call your wife, and tell her you won't be home?"

"No wife," Steve said. "Where'd you get that idea? You married?"

"Who'd have me?" Terry asked. "My sister and I live home."

"Ah, yes, Miss Fallon."

"I'll square things for you with her," Terry said. "She's really a good kid, Steve. Hard working. Loyal. That's the only reason she's sore. She likes Chennowith."

"So do I," Steve said.

The hamburgers were both huge and delicious, and after they'd eaten them, they rode back out to the plant and to the assembly line. Only one of the three lines was in operation at night, assembling four-door Crescents. Terry loaned Steve a set of coveralls, and the instruction tour began at the railway loading dock and got no farther than the placement of the frames onto the assembly line.

But, by the time they quit, Steve knew precisely how the frames were moved into position, and how each piece of the complicated process functioned. It was a good way to the other end of the assembly line, but it no longer looked to him as if he would never know how it worked.

Steve was on a metal ladder, designed for maintenance personnel, looking down at the line, watching the frames being placed into position when Fallon left him, saying he had to make a phone call. And then, all of a sudden, Howard Cole, in a smock, was on another ladder beside him.

"Looking for something?" Cole asked.

"I'm trying to see how this thing works," Steve said.

"Fallon showing you?"

"Uh huh," Steve said, wondering if Cole was going to be difficult again.

"Good man," Cole said. "He knows what he's doing," and then he climbed down off the ladder again.

Steve returned his attention to the line until Fallon reappeared. Terry put his fingers in his mouth to whistle to get Steve's attention, and then waved him off the ladder.

"That's enough for tonight, Steve," he said. "We'll pick it up tomorrow, if you like. Come on out to the house with me and meet my folks. My mother wants to meet you."

Steve really didn't want to go, but there was no way he could see to refuse without hurting Terry's feelings.

Terry's father looked very much like Terry, except that his hair was white, not red, and he was slightly larger around the middle, although Terry himself was hardly the trim-waisted soldier he'd once been. Mrs. Fallon was, Steve thought, "comfortable." She was plump, pleasant-faced and relaxed. Steve thought that she and his mother would be friends within thirty seconds of meeting one another. They were two of a kind.

Steve, from the first few words of the conversation, sensed that Terry had told his parents only that they had been in the Army together, for Mr. Fallon asked what he was doing in Atlanta.

"I was just transferred here," Steve replied, and then there was a sound from the kitchen.

"That must be my daughter, Steve," Mrs. Fallon said. "Janet, come in and meet Terry's friend."

Janet came into the room, and Steve saw that she was better dressed than she normally was at work, and that she'd even rearranged her hair. She wore a smile on her face as she walked into the room, but when she saw Steve it vanished for a moment, and then was replaced by a wide smile, very obviously phony.

"Janet," Mr. Fallon said, "This is Terry's—"

He got no further. Janet had been carrying a glass of Coke in her hand. She walked quickly to Terry and carefully poured it over his head.

"And that's not all I'm going to do to you, either," she said. "You're going to pay for this, Terry."

"Janet!" Mrs. Fallon said. "Would you mind telling me what this is all about?"

"I can't help it if she's eager, Mom," Terry said innocently. "All I did was tell the truth. I told her I was bringing home an old friend, who was not only the owner of a fancy convertible, but an engineer, and more importantly, a bachelor who didn't know any girls in Atlanta. I have no idea what happened to her."

"This," Janet said, pointing her finger at Steve, "is the man who took Mr. Chennowith's job. He's my boss."

"That's true," Terry said, obviously delighted with himself. "But he is a bachelor, and he is an engineer, and he doesn't know any girls in Atlanta. He told me so himself."

"I would like to apologize, Mr. Haas," Janet said, "for my idiot brother. He has a very peculiar sense of humor."

"I think so, too," Mrs. Fallon said. "Terry, how could you?"

"It was easy," Terry said. "She keeps bringing all

her unmarried girl friends around here, so turn
about's fair play."

"All I'm trying to do is help you," Janet said angrily.

"And what do you think I'm doing? You could do
a lot worse than Steve," Terry said. "And if I have to
have a brother-in-law, I might as well have one who
can play poker."

"I'm not surprised that he's a friend of yours," Janet blurted. "Birds of a feather—" Then she stopped.
"I'm sorry Mr. Haas," she said. "I can tell by the look
on your face that you didn't know about this."

"I think," Steve said, "that I'd better be running
along."

"I've got a better idea, Mr. Haas," Mr. Fallon said.
"I think you and I should go into the kitchen, and
have a beer, and then when these two calm down,
Terry can bring Janet in and introduce you again."

They did just that, and in a couple of minutes, Janet
looking sheepish, Terry looking anything but peni-
tent, they pushed open the swinging door.

"Steve," Terry said. "I'd like you to meet my kid
sister. Janet, this is my old buddy, Steve. And there's
a new rule. We're not going to mention Amalgamated Assembly Plant # 15 in this house. OK?"

"Hello, Janet," Steve said. "I'm happy to meet
you."

She didn't say anything for a minute, and then she
said hesitantly: "Hello, Steve. I've heard a lot about
you."

Steve thought, for the first time, that Janet Fallon
was a much better-looking girl than the one in Dallas.
She was, in fact, the best-looking girl he had seen in
a long time.

 CHAPTER EIGHT

JANET WAS IN the office when he arrived two hours late the next morning. He'd called Pickens' office and told his secretary that he would be late. He didn't give a reason, not wanting to let Pickens know that what he was doing was attending a garage sale in the housing development near Forest Wood.

He'd seen the sale advertised as he put gas in the new car, and the service station attendant told him that you could normally buy all sorts of house furnishings at a bargain at garage sales.

That had proven to be the case. At very low, almost ridiculous prices, compared to what he had paid for the bed and chair, he bought a couch, two more armchairs, a coffee table, end tables, two rugs and a set of kitchen furniture. Then he went back to the gas station, and hired the station's pickup truck and the attendant to deliver the furniture to his apartment. He would carry it up from the lobby when he got home.

When he walked into his office, Janet greeted him formally, as if she'd given some thought to the difference between the boss and his secretary, and a young man and young woman who had spent the previous evening eating pizza in her kitchen.

"Good morning, Mr. Haas," she said.

"Good morning, Miss Fallon," he said.

"Mr. Pickens' secretary told me you'd be in late," she said. "Mr. Chennowith asked me to tell you that there are no pressing problems, and that the morning meeting is scheduled for ten."

"Thank you," Steve said, adding, "Miss Fallon."

He went into his office, and in a moment, she came in and closed the door.

"I think it would be better if you called me 'Janet,' Mr. Haas," she said. "I call Mr. Chennowith 'Mr. Chennowith' and he calls me 'Janet.' "

"OK," Steve said. "I suppose we'd better, around here. But I don't think the company would collapse if I took you to dinner and the movies or something, do you?"

"I think it would probably survive," she said, with a smile.

"Tonight, I've got to arrange some furniture, which is why I was late this morning, incidentally. I just bought it. And I won't get to start that until about nine, after Terry's night school ends. But what about tomorrow night?"

"Would you like to go out double?" she asked. "With Terry and another girl?"

"Great," he said.

"I'll set it up," she said.

The intercom interrupted the conversation.

"This is Pickens," the metallic voice said. "Did Mr. Haas, by any chance, come in yet?"

"This is Haas, Mr. Pickens," Steve said.

"If you're free, Haas, would you step in for a moment?"

"Be right there, sir," Steve said.

After sending for him, Pickens kept him waiting, and when finally Steve was allowed into his office, began:

"Have you given any thought, Haas, to studying the line operation?"

"Yes, sir, I have."

"What I was thinking was that you really ought to spend some time learning the actual, physical operation of the line, before you get into anything else."

"Yes, sir, I agree," Steve said.

"In the meantime," Pickens said smoothly. "We can have Mr. Chennowith continue to exercise the responsibilities he exercised before you came."

"That won't be necessary, sir," Steve said.

"I beg your pardon?"

"I've arranged to study the line operation at night. I think I'll just sit in on the administrative meetings during the day." A worn-out cliché popped into Steve's mind, and he decided to use it. "Learn by doing, so to speak."

"Of course, that's up to you," Pickens said coldly. "Do I understand you correctly, that you have arranged to study the line operation at night?"

"Yes, sir."

"May I ask how you plan to do that?"

"One of the men is showing me the operation, sir. I figured he would know as much about it as anyone else."

"Won't that mean taking a man from his other duties?"

"No, sir, it will not."

"Someone from another shift?"

"Yes, sir."

"Now, see here, Haas, if you start something like that, you're going to get yourself involved with wages and overtime, and there's no telling how the union will react. They're liable to accuse us of attempting a speed-up."

"Oh, I don't think we'll have any trouble with the union, sir," Steve said.

"And you have reached that firm opinion on the basis of two days here?"

"The union steward is teaching me about the line, Mr. Pickens," Steve said. "And he's not being paid to do it."

"He's not being paid?" Pickens asked. "That's extraordinary."

"We're old friends, Mr. Pickens," Steve said. "He's doing it as a favor."

Pickens changed the subject.

"I understand you had a little trouble getting to work this morning. Any trouble, Mr. Haas? With your new convertible, I mean?"

"Well, the radio knob fell off," Steve said. "But that wasn't the reason I was late."

"Oh?" Pickens asked.

Steve said nothing for a long and painful pause, and then he said, "Would you like me to file a report, Mr. Pickens, of what hours I work?"

"That won't be necessary, Haas," Pickens said coldly. "Thank you for coming in."

"Thank you for thinking about me, and the line, Mr. Pickens," Steve said and left.

There was no question in his mind what Pickens was up to. If he had agreed to permit Chennowith to "exercise his responsibilities" while Steve was shown how the line worked, it would have quickly reached Detroit, rephrased: "That youngster Whitman shoved down Pickens' throat was so incompetent that they had to spend two weeks showing him what the line was, with the man he replaced doing his job for him."

He had another thought as he walked to the management team meeting. He had no right to expect Terry to give up his time to help him out. On the other hand, he couldn't offer Terry money, or Terry's feelings would be hurt. He had what he thought was a good idea. He could repay at least a little of Terry's kindness by paying for the double date the next day. But then he thought that Terry wouldn't like that either. A better solution was to have Janet and Terry and Terry's girl to his place. It was furnished now, and he could go to the supermarket and get some huge steaks. They could take a swim, too, which carried with it the additional benefit of getting a look at Janet in a bathing suit.

At the meetings he attended that day, he sat beside Chennowith, and kept his mouth firmly shut, except at the end of the first meeting of the day when he reported that it had come to his attention that a radio knob had fallen off a customer's car before the car had gone five miles.

"That sort of thing happens, Mr. Haas," one of the men spoke up, a bit of tolerance in his voice. "There's vibration on motor transporters, and even more vibration if we ship by rail. And then, of course, we don't know what has happened in the dealer's showroom. Any number of things could cause something like that."

"I suppose they could," Steve said. "But this happened to my car, and my car never even got into the transportation compound, much less on a transporter." The man colored.

"I'll check into it, Mr. Haas," he said.

Steve was torn between feeling that he'd made a

mountain out of a radio knob, and a remembered belief from the Army that the guy with the most excuses was probably the guy at fault.

Steve was thinking more and more of his Army experience. There seemed to be a number of parallels between his experience here, and the two months he'd served as first sergeant. The Army personnel system had collapsed somewhere, and failed to provide the proper number of first sergeants. Steve had been taken from his relatively comfortable duties as foreman (the Army called it Non-Commissioned Officer in Charge) of a truck overhaul facility and put into an Ordnance Ammunition Company as First Sergeant. Trucks like ammunition, were part of the Ordnance Corps, and some paper pusher had decided that was enough to consider Steve's experience as a truck mechanic sergeant as adequate to serve as an Ammo Company First Sergeant. Aside from the ammunition he used in his rifle and pistol, he knew absolutely nothing about Ordnance Ammunition; just about as much as he knew about an assembly line.

He'd felt just as helpless then as he did here. He'd survived for two months, however, by doing the best he could. And the Company Commander had told him that he'd be happy to have him stay on, even with a qualified First Sergeant now available.

Steve had gone back to his truck garage with a deep sense of relief. He didn't think he was going to be that lucky here, either in being able to learn the job as quickly as he had learned to be a First Sergeant, or in being relieved of this job and sent back to doing something he knew how to do, and liked doing.

What he had done then, he remembered, was to keep his mouth shut unless he was sure he knew what he was talking about. There were times when he'd had to take some action, make some decision, without really knowing the situation, just trusting his own judgment.

He decided now that he had, almost by accident, done the right thing to complain about something as unimportant as a loose radio knob. A customer who stepped into a brand-new Mohawk and had the radio fall apart in his hand was not only going to be annoyed, but he was going to view the whole car with suspicion, looking for other faults. Furthermore, the branch chief who had the explanations ready had the wrong attitude. What he should have done, instead of saying "Those things happen," was to find out some way to keep them from happening.

For a little while, Steve felt the first tinges of self-confidence, but they didn't last long, as he told himself that it was absurd to think that he could run the assembly line at Amalgamated Motors Company Assembly Plant # 15 as he had once run the 8435th Ordnance Ammunition Company, or the Fifth Echelon Heavy Truck Maintenance Facility.

When he met Terry at the VFW, the military thoughts returned again. There was more than a little similarity between the VFW Club and the Sergeant's Open Mess, and it was easy to wish that he was back in the Army. He'd probably be a Sergeant Major by now, if he'd stayed in, and being a Sergeant Major would have been a good deal more pleasant, and easier, than what he was doing here.

He forced himself to stop considering this by remembering that even as a Sergeant Major, he wouldn't be making half as much money—not even that much—as he was making now. There would be no brand-new, bright yellow convertible, no expensive garden apartment, no money in the bank, and, probably most important, he would have had some pimply-faced kid for a clerk-typist, instead of a rather delightful redhead.

That night, because it was on his mind, he had Terry trace for him the path of the radio on the assembly line, working backwards from the assembly line to the unloading dock. He found that even the installation of a radio in a car was more complex than it appeared on the surface. There were a number of variables. There were three kinds of radios, for one thing. The cheapest was an AM radio, and you had to dial it yourself. Next there was a radio with push-button dialing, and, most expensive, a radio which provided both the push-buttons and AM-FM reception. All models could be had with rear seat speakers, as an option. There were two different kits for rear seat speakers, one for two-door sedans and hardtops, and a second for four-door sedans. There were three kinds of antennas, a simple antenna that could be raised and lowered by hand, a power antenna and, on the top of the line, an antenna made up of gold wires invisibly sealed in the windshield.

Someone in Engineering had decided it would be cheaper to include all the wiring necessary for any variation of installation in the basic wiring harness, instead of having a separate wiring harness for each kind of installation. That explained a number of wires which had no apparent function when the car was through assembly. If there were no power antenna, for example, that wire remained unused, with an insulating cap at each end.

The punched computer card established at the beginning of assembly what speakers and which particular radio were to be put into the dashboard assembly, or—if the car was one of the rare ones which wouldn't have a radio—that the chrome filler plate for the pre-punched hole in the dash would be snapped in place. It notified the Glass Branch whether an in-the-window-antenna windshield would be required for that assembly or not. It notified the Fender & Grill Branch whether or not a hole would be required to be drilled in the right front fender, and what size hole (as the powered and standard antenna required different-sized holes). If a power antenna was to be installed, that had to be taken from stock, together with its mounting brackets, and installed.

It was nine-fifteen before Steve felt that he had at least a working knowledge of that small function of the assembly line and they could knock off for the night. Terry accepted, with seeming pleasure, the invitation for steaks the next night, admitting he was curious to see how the "rich folk" in the garden apartments lived. Terry was obviously pleased that Steve was interested in his sister, and Steve, strangely, wasn't embarrassed by this. Janet Fallon was, so far as he was concerned, the best thing Atlanta and Assembly Plant # 15 had to offer.

The furniture he had bought at the garage sale was waiting for him in the foyer of Forest Wood. Stuck to the back of the couch with a pin was an envelope with his name on it. He opened it, and found a short note from the manager: "Mr. Haas, *please* remove your property from our lobby at your *earliest* convenience."

There didn't seem to be much he could do about the couch, because obviously he couldn't handle that by himself, but he could, he thought, get the chairs and the rugs and the rest of it upstairs.

The rugs were heavier than they looked, and he stopped working when he'd carried the second one up, and sat down in his one chair with a can of beer. The door was pushed open.

"How'd you know I was going to be turned

around?" Randy Walsh asked, as he came into the room. "You psychic or something?"

"I thought you were in some exotic place like Rome or Istanbul," Steve said. "Want a beer?"

"I'd love a beer," Walsh said, and helped himself. "I got caught. They turned me around."

"I don't understand that," Steve said.

"Well, the FAA sets the maximum number of hours we can fly in a month. What I try to do is get them in just as quick as I can, because then I'm free. Most of the other guys are married, and they're perfectly willing to have me take their trips when their wives want to go some place, or the kid is having a birthday or something. But the airline likes us to space our flight hours. I got caught in London. They sent me right back. I'll go out again in about three days."

"Well, I'm glad you're here," Steve said. "I need a strong back. I got a little note from the manager telling me to get my junk out of the foyer."

"Doesn't look like it's junk," Randy said. "Where'd you get it?"

"A garage sale, on the way to work this morning," Steve said. "I didn't think I could exist on a bed and one chair and your TV tables."

"I would have carried it up, but your door was locked," Randy said. "You on the night shift, or have you found some kindred soul with whom to while away your leisure hours?"

"I don't suppose you'd be interested," Steve said. "But tonight I became a quick expert on the installation of radios in automobiles. Tomorrow night, I learn how they put air conditioners on. No. Not tomorrow night."

"What happens tomorrow night?" Randy asked, naturally.

"To tell the truth, I'm taking the night off. I'm

going to have a party. Why don't you come and bring a girl? I make a fine steak."

"I accept," Randy said. "I'll put a note on the bulletin board, announcing that I am home and available, and that applications may be made from 7 until 8 tomorrow morning."

"Make it ten to eleven," Steve said, laughing. "Sleep late."

"I have a big date tomorrow morning," Randy said. "An expensive one."

"Huh?"

"I've got a Warrior hardtop I run in the Grand American Challenge," Randy said. "I'm going to put a new carburetor on it."

"I know what a Warrior is," Steve said. "But what's the Grand American Challenge?"

"Used to be called Grand Touring," Randy said. "NASCAR changed the name to Grand American Challenge. You know, auto racing."

"Sure," Steve said. "I guess I should have known."

"Why?" Randy asked.

"I'm in the automobile business," Steve said.

"Is that so? What do you do?"

"I put Warriors together, as a matter of fact," Steve said.

"Really? You mean you stand there with an impact wrench in your hands and bolt the fenders on?"

"Well, sort of," Steve said. "I run the assembly line. Or I will, when I learn what it's all about."

"That's what you meant by being a rádio installation expert?"

"Yeah."

"I'm impressed," Randy said. "Do you suppose you can get me parts wholesale?"

"I don't know," Steve said. "I'll find out. I don't see why not. I just got a car wholesale."

"Is that yellow convertible yours? I saw it when I came in just now."

"Yeah."

"Brand new, isn't it?"

"So new the radio knob fell off," Steve said. Randy looked at him curiously. "Forget it. Private joke," Steve said.

"Come on, I'll help you carry your stuff up."

"I'm grateful," Steve said. "I don't want the manager sore at me so soon after I've moved in."

"I have an ulterior motive," Randy said, and Steve wasn't sure if he was entirely joking. "I need access to wholesale parts. I sometimes think it would be cheaper to give up racing and get married."

They weren't very clever about moving the furniture. They carried it all up the stairs and into the apartment, and only then remembered that the rugs were still lying rolled against the wall. They had to carry all the living room furniture and then the bedroom furniture, out onto the balcony, unroll the rugs, and then carry the furniture back in.

But the result, Steve decided when he looked around his living room, was well worth the effort. He found it difficult to believe that it was really his; it looked more like an advertisement in a magazine than a place where he actually lived.

Randy broke in the couch by kicking off his loafers, lying down on it, and ordering Steve to deliver a beer.

It was long after midnight before Randy walked across the patio to his own apartment. Steve couldn't remember what they'd talked about for so long, but he did think that it had been a long time since he'd just sat around talking with someone his own age. He decided that things were looking up all over.

CHAPTER NINE

ONE OF THE documents which had passed over Steve's desk the day before had been a company form announcing the arrival of a trainload of engines. It had been precise. The train would arrive at 5:30 in the morning. Steve set his alarm for quarter to five, and was on the platform when the yard engine pushed in the string of boxcars.

It was a clever and well-planned operation. The engines were each on a small wooden pallet, and four pallets were strapped together with steel banding, making one load for a fork-lift truck. The fork-lift truck drove into each boxcar, picked up a load, and carried it a short distance into the plant. There the bands were cut, and the engines carried off individually by a conveyor.

The larger pallets were collected, and loaded into

the first off-loaded boxcar for return to the engine assembly plant. Steve saw that as each engine went past one of the administrative offices, a man removed from it still another computer card. He was just slightly pleased with himself when he found out, by asking, that what the card did (adjust the in-plant inventory, and locate that particular engine) was what he had thought it would.

The operation looked complicated, but the closer he got to it, the more he sensed that despite its seeming complexity, it was really a very logical, easy-to-understand process.

He had breakfast in the canteen, and was in his office at quarter to eight. As he didn't think it was necessary to tell Mr. Pickens he had arrived at the plant at 5:25, he didn't think it was necessary for him to tell Mr. Pickens he was taking off for the day at 3:40, which was when the final meeting of the day would be adjourned. It didn't even occur to him that he had been at work for more than ten hours.

For some reason, shortly after lunch, as he watched in fascination the upholstery assemblers put seats together, he remembered that he had neither china nor silverware to feed six people, and that there had been just one can of beer left in his refrigerator when Randy had gone home.

In downtown Atlanta, he found a set of china at what he felt was a reasonable price and twenty minutes later, a set of silverplate which cost what he considered an outrageous price. But he had to have it, and he bought it.

Then he stopped by the supermarket and bought the meat. His mother's husband, who owned his own butcher shop, had given him a valuable tip. Butchers, like anyone else with a skill, have pride in their work. Supermarket butchers often spend their whole work day without a word of appreciation from their customers, who just pick up pre-packaged meat from the display cooler.

It worked here, too. Steve pushed the button marked "Personal Service," told the butcher who came out the truth, that he wanted some steaks to impress a girl, and received steaks that were obviously more attractive than those on display. And the butcher was obviously pleased when Steve told him that it was good-looking meat.

There wasn't much time to prepare the meal even though he'd taken off early; and he was relieved when Terry called to say there was no reason for him to pick up Janet. Terry would "drag her along" and Steve could take her home later, if he wanted to.

At half past seven, precisely on time, the doorbell rang. It was the first time Steve had heard it, and he was pleased. It was a four-tone chime, instead of a buzzer.

When it rang, his hands were covered with bacon grease, with which he was preparing the skin of the baked potatoes, so he just called out:

"Door's open, come on in." He heard the door open, heard the sound of footsteps which sounded feminine, and called, "In the kitchen."

Behind him, a very low voice said, "Hi, I hope I'm in the right place."

He turned and found himself looking at a strikingly beautiful girl. She looked like she belonged in the movies.

"I hope you are too," he said. "I'm Steve Haas."

"Randy called," she said. "He'll be a little late. He said I should meet him here." She put out her hand. "I'm Eloise Higgins." Steve forgot that his hands were greasy and took it.

She looked at her hand with shock. It was shiny with bacon grease.

"Sorry," Steve said. "I didn't think."

"No harm," she said, taking the paper towel he offered her hurriedly.

"The others'll be here in a minute," Steve said.

"Can I get you a beer?"

"Ruins my figure," she said. "You don't happen to have a glass of wine?"

He didn't have any wine. That was the second thing he'd done wrong. He was really impressed with Eloise's good looks, but, considering Randy, not really very surprised. Randy could almost be expected to know girls like this one.

He decided that when the others arrived, he'd run out and get some wine. He should have thought of that.

Terry and Janet and Terry's date, a brunette girl named Margaret, came next. Terry had brought with him half a case of beer. Steve compared Janet with Eloise, and decided that what really made Eloise so striking was her clothes and hairdo. Janet was more simply dressed.

"The last time I was in Steve's living quarters," Terry said, "he was considered well off because he had his own chair. He's come up in the world."

Randy Walsh appeared ten minutes later. First, he stuck his head in the door, just long enough to let everyone see that he was dirty, sweaty and grease-stained.

"Is this the place where the man from Amalgamated Motors lives?" he asked.

"I don't think I'm going to like this," Steve said. Randy disappeared and then reappeared, kicking the door open and walking directly to Steve. He was as dirty all over as he was on his face. He was wearing torn and stained Levis, and an even dirtier work shirt with the name of his airline on it.

"Here you go, buddy," he said to Steve and handed him something, so quickly that Steve took it without thinking. It was a carburetor, complete except for the air filter. It was greasy. "You make lousy automobiles, you know that?" Randy said. "Now, if you'll excuse me, I'll go wash some of this muck off."

And with that, he was gone.

"What's that thing?" Eloise asked.

"Carburetor," Terry said, and walked over to look at it. The casting at the bottom was broken.

"Who was that?" Janet asked.

"Randy Walsh," Steve said. "My neighbor. He works for the airline."

"I saw the shirt," Janet said.

"I knew his important business," Eloise said, "was that ridiculous automobile."

"What's he do," Terry asked, "race it?"

"Unsuccessfully," Eloise said, "but with great determination."

The carburetor was taken into the kitchen, and set on the sink.

"Over-torqued it," Terry said professionally. "Look at the way it cracked."

"Looks that way," Steve agreed.

"I knew it," Janet said. "I just knew it."

"Knew what?"

"That we would spend the evening talking either about automobiles or the Army."

"If you've got anything bright to say about, say, flower arranging or the political situation," Terry said, "I'm perfectly willing to listen."

Janet turned away from them and spoke to Eloise. "Do you work here in Atlanta?" she asked.

Eloise nodded. "At Rich's," she said. "I'm a model." That, Steve figured, figured. He couldn't quite picture Eloise punching a typewriter in an office.

"I work for Steve," Janet said. "Out at Amalgamated."

"I thought we weren't going to talk about automobiles," Margaret, Terry's date, said.

Randy reappeared in an astonishingly short time, freshly showered, carrying two bottles, and wearing a yellow turtleneck and a yellow nylon zipper jacket with a picture of a horse and the words: CIRCLE HIPPIQUE, KINSHASA.

"Some French grape juice," he said. "I thought it might come in handy."

"What's that on the jacket?" Janet asked.

"You get stuck in the Congo for at least 24 hours," Randy said. "Sometimes as much as 72 hours between planes. This is the horse club. Best place in town to wait."

"I thought you were a mechanic," Janet said.

"And I thought you were going to bring me perfume from Paris," Eloise said. "You promised and promised."

"I only got as far as London," Randy said to Eloise, and then, to Janet, "I'm a pretty good mechanic." He turned again to Steve. "And I torqued that lousy carburetor to within an ounce of 35 pounds. What's it supposed to be?"

Steve had no idea, but Terry answered: "Thirty to forty pounds, according to specs. You sure?"

"I'm positive," Randy said. "That's a faulty part."

"There's generally," Steve said, "at least a 25% allowance on torque stress, and it doesn't seem likely that a torque wrench would be that much in error."

"I can *feel* thirty pounds of torque," Randy said. "It boils down to the fact that you guys build lousy cars."

"You're a mechanic for the airline, are you?" Janet asked.

"No, not really," Randy said. "More like a bus driver. But that's got nothing to do with my ability as a mechanic."

"Steve," Terry said, "we've got a magnaflux machine out there. You want to take that out with you in the morning and see what's wrong with it? If he's sure it was properly torqued—"

"I thought we agreed we weren't going to talk about automobiles," Janet said.

"That's a fine idea," Randy said. "But let's not talk about airlines either, OK? Or where they go? Or anything like that?"

"If you think you have enough mechanical ability to get the cork out of one of those bottles," Eloise said. "I could drink a glass, and if I have a glass of wine, I won't keep reminding you that I didn't get the perfume you promised from Paris."

"I told you," Randy said. "I only got as far as London."

"You travel quite a bit, do you, in your line of work?" Janet asked.

"Well, I'll tell you, Red," Randy said. "When they have your picture hanging on every Post Office bulletin board, you have to keep moving."

"I think I'll start the steaks," Steve said.

The steaks were as good as they looked, and by all standards but one, the party was a success. Before it was over, of course, Janet had learned that Randy was an airlines pilot, assigned to international flights, and just as predictably, Randy had promised to bring Janet perfume, too, the next time he went to Paris.

Randy's date hadn't been jealous, because she had had no reason to be. Randy obviously understood Steve's interest in Janet, and was treating her with the cool and distant attitude with which a nice guy treats his buddy's girl friend.

Steve, however, saw that in Janet's eyes, a pilot flying to Europe and the Congo had far more glamour than he could muster as the none-too-expert manager of an auto assembly line.

At seven-fifteen the next morning, Steve was in the quality control laboratory of the plant, carrying the cracked carburetor housing in newspaper. The technician on duty was very pleasant and helpful, and soon had the casting in place to be magnafluxed. The testing showed no manufacturing imperfections.

"It looks to me, Mr. Haas," he said, "as if it was put on by somebody who wasn't a mechanic, and it was over-torqued."

Steve fought down the temptation to agree with the technician. It would have been nice to be able to tell Terry and Janet, as well as Randy, that the broken part was Randy's own fault. But he didn't honestly think that was the case.

"Have you got the necessary material to ship that to Detroit?" Steve asked.

"Sure."

"Send it to Engineering," Steve said. "I'll put a letter in the mail. We'll see what they have to say about it."

When he reached his office, and sat down at Janet's typewriter, he thought about the proper way to bring the matter to the attention of the proper people. He was no longer a supervisory engineer, directly responsible to Stuart Whitman. If he were, he would have written a short note to Bob Hyneman, in charge of the cast metallurgy laboratory, "See what busted this, will you, please, and let me know?"

Instead, he wrote Whitman a fairly formal letter and told him, formally, that the defective part had been brought to his attention by a dissatisfied customer, and that he felt the customer's statement that the assembly had been bolted in place with the recommended torque, to be actually the case. He signed himself, naturally, "Steve," but he wrote his first name over the more formal title, "Manager, Assembly Line, Assembly Plant #15."

He had just folded the letter and sealed it in an envelope when Pickens walked in.

"Oh, good morning, Haas," he said.

"Good morning, Mr. Pickens," Steve said.

"In a little early, aren't you?" Pickens remarked.

"I had a letter to write," Steve replied.

"So I see," Pickens said. "Do you habitually type your own letters?"

"Sometimes," Steve said. "When my secretary isn't around."

"How's your familiarity with the line progressing?" Pickens asked.

"It's coming along," Steve said. "I'm beginning to make some sense out of it."

"Well, I'll see you at the meeting," Pickens said, and left. Steve looked at the closed door for some time after Pickens had left. He didn't think that Pickens made a habit of visiting other offices before the work day began. He hadn't said what was on his mind. On the other hand, he had, Steve remembered, taken a long and careful look at the envelope addressed to "Mr. Stuart Whitman, Vice President, Engineering, Amalgamated Motors Corporation, Detroit, Michigan."

Pickens probably thought Steve was writing Whitman behind his back, about the plant. That was a shame, but on the other hand, what was Pickens doing snooping in his office a half hour before Janet was supposed to be there?

After lunch, he saw Terry on the assembly line and told him the results of the magnaflux testing.

"I sent it to Detroit," Steve said. "I think Randy put it on properly."

"If you're really curious, Steve," Terry said, "we could watch him put one on."

"I'll get one from stock," Steve said, "and we'll go there when you quit for the day."

"And we can come out here again, afterward," Terry said.

Before the afternoon meeting, Steve had Janet make up a requisition for a carburetor (officially known as Assembly, Carburetor, Four Barrel, with mounting bolts, less air-cleaner assembly, Part No. 73-4002-344) from stock, signed it, and asked her to see that it was in the office when the meeting was over.

"For Randy?" she asked.

"Yeah," Steve said. "Terry and I are either going to put it on ourselves, or watch him, to see that he puts it on properly." Then, not really knowing why, he added, "You want to come along?"

"I don't think I should," she said. "But I'd like to. I've never seen a racing car up close."

"Come along, then," Steve said. He had the feeling that she was really more interested in seeing Randy than his engine block, but on the other hand, she would at least learn that he knew as much about cars as her brother did. He realized that he wanted to show off a little in front of Janet, and he felt like a fool.

When the three of them reached Forest Wood, Randy was at the pool, stretched out on an aluminum chair. Steve had to admit Randy was a good-looking guy, with a warm smile, who would obviously appeal to girls.

"Not only do you make lousy parts," Randy greeted them, "but you have a lousy distribution system. The parts house says they'll have to have my carburetor sent in from New York. I told him I had highly placed friends at the assembly plant, but it didn't make much of an impression."

"We brought you a carburetor," Steve said. "The magnaflux machine showed no structural faults in yours."

"You also brought Janet," Randy said, beaming at her. "Thank you for both."

"You're welcome," Terry said drily. "Where is this wreck of yours? We'll show you how to put it on right."

"Wait till I put some clothes on," Randy said, "and I'll be right with you."

Randy had two adjacent garages in the rear of Forest Wood. He had removed the partition separating the garages, and there was enough room for a not too crowded working garage.

Steve was honest enough to admit that he liked the cleanliness and order in the garage. Randy had mounted pegboards to the partitions and the concrete block back wall, and he had an impressive array of good quality tools, all clean and in place.

The car, a Mohawk Warrior hardtop, bore the number 91 on the sides of the car, the roof, and on the trunk lid. The headlight holes had been filled in with round sheets of aluminum. Inside there were a number of obvious changes. The rear seats were gone, and the front seat replaced with a sturdy bucket seat for the driver alone. There was a heavy roll-bar arrangement, and the floorboard showed where a reinforcement had been installed to protect the driver, in case the clutch or flywheel disintegrated.

There were thick racing tires, with a 10-inch tread, on all four wheels, and, although it didn't show, the gas tank had been replaced with a fuel cell which would not rupture in a crash.

Steve, because he was interested in racing generally, had read the NASCAR Rule Book, and realized that the rules had been designed to keep the car, if not as nearly "stock" as possible, from being a machine entirely converted to high speed racing, as the NASCAR Grand National cars were built. He remembered that NASCAR insisted that the standard ignition system be used, and even that the driveshaft, universals and flywheel must be the kind provided by the factory for regular cars.

Grand American Challenge, he knew, had been established by NASCAR so that amateur, or semi-professional drivers could race. Grand National racing, where the cars cost upwards of $25,000, eliminated all racers but the professionals.

"Don't you guys want to change your clothes?" Randy asked, as Terry began to take the carburetor from its box.

"All we're going to do is put on a carburetor," Terry said. "And we like to think of ourselves as professionals."

"I'll take off my jacket," Steve said, "just to keep my cuffs away from that filthy engine block."

"Don't mind them," Janet said to Randy. "They're just insufferably smug."

"I'll withhold judgment until I see if it runs," Randy said.

Without actually saying anything, Terry and Steve agreed to show them how quickly a carburetor could be installed and adjusted. Terry put the carburetor in place with a facility only someone who has installed literally thousands of identical carburetors on identical engines could possibly have. His hands seemed to be doing two or more separate things at once. Then he stepped back, with all the lines connected, and let Steve take over.

Terry reached into the passenger compartment and switched the engine on, and then Steve bent over the carburetor with a screwdriver and made the final adjustments. The engine purred smoothly and powerfully, and the job hadn't taken them in all, more than five minutes.

"That ought to do it," Terry said grandly. "It's

idling a little rough, but that's not the fault of the carburetor."

"OK, you guys," Randy said. "I'm impressed. But I still swear I didn't over-torque those bolts."

"We'll find out," Steve said. "The old carburetor's on its way to the engineering labs in Detroit."

"Let's take it out to the track and see what it does," Randy said. "Janet, would you like to see that?"

"I'd love to," she said. "It sounds fascinating."

"OK, then?"

"I've got nightschool, unfortunately," Steve said. "Some other time."

"All work and no play, and so on, makes Jack you know what," Randy said.

"Maybe over the weekend," Steve said.

"Saturday morning," Randy said. "We could go get a pizza, or something, Janet, while these two are off at hard work."

"All right," she said. "And then you'll show us how it runs on Saturday?"

"That I will," Randy said. "I've been scheduled for a flight Saturday night, but there will be time."

CHAPTER TEN

ON FRIDAY NIGHT, when Steve and Terry left the plant long after nine o'clock, they stopped in at the VFW for a beer, and stayed until the place closed. Since he was dressed to crawl around the assembly line, rather than to sit behind a desk in the administrative building, the other members of the VFW, many of them assembly plant employees, accepted Steve as one more assembler, who had been in the Army with Terry.

The VFW Club had a pool table, and Steve spent most of the evening playing 8-Ball. He enjoyed the people in the club, and he enjoyed the prospect of the weekend off. He was developing an understanding of the assembly line, to the point where he at least understood what the management people were talking about when they raised problems, real and potential, at the management meetings. The rather unpleasant feeling of being entirely over his depth was ever more quickly dissipating. He was beginning to understand that he wasn't supposed to be able to design and plan the operation of the assembly line, but rather to see that it ran efficiently.

What had looked to be an operation completely impossible to master, was coming into focus. He didn't even have to order parts; others were responsible for that. As he came to understand the job, he came to understand that it wasn't that much of a responsibility, either. He was, in one sense, just a man with an oilcan, keeping his part of a huge system going.

The decisions he was asked to make weren't at all monumental, or even very important, compared with the decisions people like Whitman had to make. Assembly Plant #15 was not only told that it was to make a certain number of cars, but told what model cars, and at what rate of speed. Pickens' decision was to determine how many assembly lines would be required to make that many cars. Steve's decisions (now being made by Chennowith in his name) were very low level, very practical. He had to decide whether such and such piece of equipment had gone through its useful life and should be replaced, rebuilt, or kept in use a little longer. He had to decide when was the best time to shut down one line for preventative maintenance, shifting assembly operations to another line while that was being done. The most important decisions he had watched Chennowith make were labor relations decisions, whether to give in to a complaint from one of the shop stewards as valid, or whether to fight it. If he decided to fight it, the decision-making process moved up to the Vice President, Administration, and then to Pickens, so even that wasn't much of a responsibility.

Steve had formed a somewhat irreverent opinion of labor-management relations even before he'd come to Atlanta. He was convinced that both sides in the never-ending battle between them played sort of a game. One side made an outrageous demand against the other, fully expecting an outrageous counter proposal. After they had huffed and puffed at each other for a while, they would come to a reasonably fair agreement. If one side gained an advantage in one controversy, it was a good bet that the other side would get the advantage in the next bargaining session.

He had already formed the somewhat immodest idea that he was going to have less trouble dealing with the union than Chennowith did, for the very good reason that the shop stewards were people like Terry, which was the same thing as saying people like himself. They understood each other. Chennowith, through no fault of his own, looked like a boss, and people just don't like bosses.

The blunt fact underlying the whole labor-management arrangement was that both had an interest in keeping the assembly line moving. While a union work stoppage or even a strike certainly hurt the company, it also hurt the strikers, who didn't get paid if they were on strike.

When he got home that night, he saw a U-Drive-It pickup truck parked in front of Randy Walsh's garage, beside a one-car-capacity trailer. It would be fun, he thought, going to a race track tomorrow with Randy. Somewhat smugly, he wasn't at all displeased with the thought that while Randy might own the car, and thereby impress Janet, his knowledge of high performance engines was greater than Randy's, and he might come out looking just a little better than Randy.

Randy was in a very good mood in the morning,

too. He knocked at Steve's door very early, and cooked them a breakfast of steak and eggs. He was wearing khaki pants, a T shirt and his *Circle Hippique Kinshasa* zipper jacket. He was carrying a set of fire-resistant racing coveralls and a racing helmet. The coveralls were lettered RANDY WALSH, and the helmet just RANDY.

"Do you suppose, now that I've put your car back together for you, that I could take a lap in it?" Steve asked, as he stacked the breakfast dishes in the sink.

"I'd be happy to let you, Steve," Randy said. "But you have to have a special kind of license. A racing license."

"Issued by whom?" Steve asked innocently.

"Well, primarily by NASCAR," Randy said. "You'd have to have a NASCAR license to race."

"Well, how would I get a NASCAR license?"

"Take the test, be examined; it's a fairly complex procedure, frankly," Randy said, and Steve suspected he rather enjoyed this routine of "I can play, but you can't."

"You don't suppose an FIA license would be accepted, do you?" Steve asked with a bright smile.

"I'm sure it would," Randy replied without thinking, then: "You just don't happen to have an FIA license, do you?"

"Yes, I do," Steve said. "Wait till I get my stuff, and then we can go pick up Terry."

He went into the bedroom and brought out his helmet and racing suit, laid it on the couch, and then went back into his bedroom. He peeked through the crack in the door to see Randy get quickly to his feet, unfold Steve's racing suit and read what was embroidered on it: "HAWKE RACING TEAM—*Steve Haas.*" He folded it again and was sitting innocently in the armchair when Steve came back in the room.

"OK," he said. "Where'd you get the costume?"

"My first job with Amalgamated was with the Hawke team," Steve said.

"Do much driving?" Randy asked.

"Well," Steve said, just as falsely modest as Randy had been, "I test drove the Hawke Model 19, of course."

"Did you? Ever race it?"

"No," Steve said. "I used to run an Osca. Nurnburgring, for example." He paused. "Willi Faust set it up for me."

He reasoned that if Randy knew anything at all about European road racing, he would recognize Willi Faust's name. From the look on his face, Steve saw that he had guessed right.

The truth wasn't nearly as impressive as Steve was letting Randy think it was. He had raced the Osca only a half dozen times, and hadn't done well at all. The fact that Willi Faust had set it up for him had been a coincidence. Willi, when Steve had met him, had been in temporary retirement from the racing garages, operating a regular garage in Marburg, where Steve had gone to school. He hadn't known that Willi was a famous racing mechanic until long after he'd exchanged his labor for the use of Willi's garage and tools. Willi had set up the Osca to keep his hand in, rather than because he thought Steve was a first-rate driver, deserving of his mechanical skill.

But, Steve reasoned, since he hadn't actually lied about it, there seemed to be no harm in letting Randy sweat a little, especially since he had been so eager to impress Janet with his being a racing driver in addition to the glamor of being an airlines pilot.

With something close to delight, Steve drove home the sword. "I'll go get Janet and Terry," he said. "I don't think Janet would like to ride in the dirty pickup truck, do you?"

"No, I don't suppose she would," Randy said rapidly

"I'll give you a hand, Randy, to get the car on the trailer, and then we'll meet you out there."

They smiled broadly and insincerely at each other, and then they both laughed genuinely.

"I'll have to remember not to underestimate you, Steve," Randy said.

"Whatever do you mean?" Steve asked innocently.

The Atlanta International Speedway was a large and impressive track. The guard at the gate to the infield, reached through a tunnel under the track itself, wouldn't let them in without paying standard admission, but suggested that if they were going to meet a race driver, he probably would have made arrangements for them at the Administration Office.

They ran into another obstacle here. Janet, as the guest of a car owner, could go into the infield, but women were barred from the pits, and there were no exceptions. Janet, predictably, was annoyed.

Steve was given a temporary license, and, in exchange for twenty-dollars, was told that NASCAR would honor his FIA license, and he would be sent one in the mail.

"I can't drive, and she can't even watch," Steve said. "Great beginning."

If he had hoped to impress Janet with his racing credentials, he failed. She seemed to think that there was no basic difference between a state driver's license and any other.

Now equipped with credentials, they passed under the track and drove past the pits. Steve was able to park the car so that Janet could sit on the hood and see what was happening in the pits through the hurricane fence separating the infield from the track.

There was no racing scheduled for the day, but both Grand American Challenge and Grand National Races would be held the following weekend, and there were cars and crews and drivers preparing for that.

It was some distance from where Steve left Janet sitting on the parked car, along the fence, through the pit gate and back to Randy's pit, and when Steve and Terry got there, Randy was talking to Janet through the fence.

"I wonder which one's feeding the other one the peanuts?" Terry asked, "despite the sign, 'Please don't feed the monkey'?"

Janet didn't think her brother was at all funny.

Randy strapped on his helmet and climbed into his racing suit and fired up the Warrior. Steve listened carefully to the sound of the engine, and had to admit that it sounded good. Terry apparently didn't think so. He went to a tool kit in the back of the pickup truck, opened the hood and made adjustments to the carburetor.

Then Randy pulled the shoulder straps into his lap, fastened them, tapped the accelerator, and let out the clutch. He fishtailed a little moving down the access road to the track, in low, and was almost wound up in second before he entered the track itself.

He took three laps, each a little faster than the previous lap, and then turned off onto the pit road again, revving the engine as he coasted to a stop in neutral.

"There's a stopwatch board in the pickup," Randy said. "You want to time me a couple of laps? Start with the third one."

Steve went to the truck and got the board. It held three stopwatches, a pencil on a string, a pad of paper, and an elapsed time chart for the Atlanta track, converting, in seconds to the third decimal point, the time it took to make a loop of the track, into miles per hour.

He walked to the fence, and Janet got off the hood of his car, and he showed her how the timing board worked. When Randy passed their position, Steve would push the buttons starting two of the watches. When the car had completed a lap, he would push one stopwatch button again, stopping that watch, and simultaneously start the third watch. While Randy was making his second lap, he would write down the time from the stopped watch, and reset it. When Randy completed his second lap, Steve would push the first watch again, starting it again, as he stopped the third watch. The watch in the middle, which ran for as long as Randy was being timed, could be used to check the time, by comparing the total time elapsed on it against the sum of the other times.

When Randy came around the final turn before the start-finish straightaway, he was moving very fast. The sound of the engine was deep and loud and even angry. Janet was obviously thrilled.

When the first lap was completed, her eyes widened when she saw the time conversion: 146.550 miles per hour. The second timed lap was even faster: 148.275. On the third lap, trying to better even that, Randy wobbled going into the first turn, and had to take up more of the track than he wanted to, to retain control, enough to lower his third lap time to 145.890.

"I've never seen a car go that fast before," Janet said. "That's very impressive."

"Yes, it is," Steve said, and one part of his brain told him that it was absolutely childish of him to plan to show her how fast he would take that car around, while another part of his brain welcomed the opportunity.

Randy came in on the next lap, shutting off the engine as he entered the pit access road, and then looking genuinely surprised after he'd crawled out of the car and examined the speeds.

"That's not bad at all," he said. He let Steve sweat a good three minutes before he asked, all sweetness and light, "Would you like to take a couple of laps, Steve, to see how she runs?"

"I wouldn't mind, if you think it would be all right," Steve said.

"Just make a little effort, Steve," Randy said, "to stay on the black stuff, will you?"

Janet giggled.

"Janet, would you get my suit and hard hat out of the back seat, please?" Steve asked, and, on the third try, she managed to throw both over the fence.

Randy made a pretty good show of explaining to Steve how the car worked, with Janet an appreciative audience. Then Randy stepped away and picked up the stopwatch board. Terry stuck his head in the window as Steve was adjusting the shoulder straps.

"One thing to keep in mind, Steve," he said seriously.

"What's that?" Steve asked.

"You're going to have to decide whether impressing Janet is worth what bouncing this thing off the guard rails would cost you. I'd say he's got six thousand, maybe more, tied up in this heap."

"I'll be careful, buddy," Steve said. "What makes you think I'm trying to impress Janet?"

Terry laughed out loud. Steve angrily pushed the starter switch and was pleased when the engine caught immediately, because the noise drowned out Terry's derisive laughter.

He tapped the accelerator several times and watched the tachometer jump. Then, with the gear shift in neutral, he worked the clutch several times to get the feel of its spring pressure. It was stiff, requiring a good deal of pressure, far more than on a European road-racing car. More weight was being moved with this car than with an Osca or the Hawke Model 19, by a far more powerful engine. The clutch pressure had to be greater.

Then he depressed the clutch and moved the gear shift lever through the gears. There was a sloppiness, he felt, to the linkage that should be corrected. But it wasn't nearly as important in a track car like this one, where once you were in upper gear, you stayed there most of the time. In road racing, you practically rowed it along with the gear shift, going down in the gears as often as you went up. There, short, precise linkage was essential.

He ran his eyes over the dials in front of him one final time, pressed on the accelerator, let out the clutch, moved four feet in three jumps, and stalled out.

Terry applauded loudly. "Attaboy, Steve baby! Show us how it's done."

Steve pressed the starter switch again and pumped the accelerator once, and the engine caught again. The moment he thought it had smoothed down enough, he pressed much harder on the accelerator and let the clutch out. He heard the squeal of rubber beneath the car. It fishtailed, and he quickly went into second, too fast. The car jumped and bucked, and for a moment he was afraid that he was going to stall it out again. If he did that, he realized, Randy would have every excuse in the world to come over and explain how to start it. Or even throw him out from behind the wheel.

But the tremendous engine power came through, and the car seemed to settle toward the rear as the tachometer needle began to climb. Steve passed onto the track itself, ran the engine revolutions up some more, and then, judging by the seat of his pants, rather than by the tachometer, shifted into high.

Almost immediately he was into the first turn, and he felt the centrifugal force of the banked curves pushing him against the seat. There was no speedometer, and he couldn't tell how fast he was going by using the tachometer, but he felt that he was doing seventy-five, maybe eighty miles an hour. He stayed in the center of the track until he was through the turn and then, on the rear straightaway, tested the steering and suspension by veering from one side of the track to the other.

He entered the second turn doing, he felt, maybe 90 miles an hour, and tested the handling under the banked-turn conditions. He went past the pits slowly enough, at just under 100 miles per hour, to get a quick glimpse of someone in a racing suit (obviously Randy) standing next to a girl (obviously Janet) at the fence.

With more than a little effort, Steve resisted shoving his foot to the floor. He would make the wrong kind of an impression on Janet if he were to lose control of this machine by being too eager to show off in front of her before he knew the track.

He made five laps of the track, and then, as he entered the start-finish straightaway, he saw Randy standing on the concrete block wall, making "Come In" signs. Instead, he put his foot to the floor, and as he went past Randy, he took both hands off the wheel and pointed with the index finger of his right hand to the wrist watch on his left wrist: "Time me."

He knew he was moving fast now by the additional pressure forcing him downward against the seat as he went around the first turn. The tachometer was indicating 5,750 revolutions as he went down the rear straightaway, and he felt the steering grow heavy in the second turn. Coming out of it, he half expected to see Randy waving him in again, but Randy wasn't visible in the flicker he had of the pits at that speed.

Three-quarters of the way down the start-finish straightaway, at the moment he eased off very lightly on the accelerator, he had the feeling that he was running flat out, that he was experiencing the first symptoms of valve-float.

Going down the rear straightaway, the suspicion became fact. He was experiencing valve-float. He looked at the tach. The needle was just past 6,000 revolutions per minute, maybe 6,100. The engine shouldn't be flat out at that speed. It lost power, the car slowed, and then picked it up again after Steve decreased pressure on the accelerator. It ran well at just under 6,000 rpm.

He took two more laps, paying more attention to valve-float than trying to set a speed that would beat Randy's. On this track, he realized that he could, if the engine would let him, go a good deal faster than he had gone.

Finally, halfway through the second turn on the third lap, he lowered the pressure on the accelerator, swept wide, and then pulled into the access road. He shut off the ignition and depressed the clutch and rolled to a stop.

There were a half dozen other men, all beaming broadly, in the pits. Randy didn't look too cheerful.

Terry walked to the car.

"Can I have my crow roasted," he asked. "Or do I have to eat it raw?"

"Your feeble little brain is trying to tell me something, I know," Steve said.

"Were you flat out?"

"I got floating valves at six thousand, or a little above," Steve said, as he pulled off his gloves and then his helmet.

"You were going as fast as it would go, then?"

"Yeah. What was I turning?"

"One sixty-two something, as an average. On the second timed lap, you did one sixty-six."

Now the men who hadn't been in the pit when he left gathered around the car, all smiles, congratulations, and eager to help.

"That's the way, Mr. Haas," one said. Another said, "Hand me the hat, Mr. Haas." Another: "Let me give you a hand, Mr. Haas." And still another: "It's great to see you out here, Mr. Haas."

"I have the feeling I'm being put on," Steve said. "Who are you guys?"

"Why, we're from the plant, Mr. Haas," one of them said. "Good old Assembly Plant Fifteen." One by one, they put out their hands, and introduced themselves.

"The thing is, Steve," Terry said, "some of the fellas are interested in racing, and, well, I let them know we'd be out here today."

"We'd like to talk to you about racing sometime, Mr. Haas," one of them said. "Sometime when you've got a couple of free minutes at the plant."

"Sure," Steve said, not wanting to sound rude. "But I'm not much of a—"

"How 'bout Monday morning, at the 9:15 break?" the man pursued. "Either at your office, or in the canteen?"

"I have the feeling I have just been took," Steve said, but he said it with a smile. "OK. I'll see you for coffee at 9:15."

Terry looked so positively angelic that there was no question whatever in Steve's mind that whatever was going on, Terry was at the bottom of it.

But now, so to speak, was his moment of glory with Janet. He'd not only beaten Randy's time, but by fifteen miles an hour.

"Very impressive," Randy said, when Steve walked over to where he stood with Janet.

"You're more of a gentleman than I would be, Randy" Janet said, almost angrily.

"Huh?" Steve said.

"I think you ought to be ashamed of yourself," Janet said. "Taking somebody else's car and driving it that crazily."

Randy took the opportunity. With a straight face, he said, "Yes, Steve, really, if I'd known you were going to drive it that fast, I wouldn't have let you have a chance at the wheel."

"I'll bet you wouldn't," Steve said.

"You could apologize," Janet said.

"I apologize for driving your car fifteen miles an hour faster than you drove it," Steve said, smiling from ear to ear.

"Well," Randy said, "as long as you don't make a *habit* of it."

"Randy's going to show me the inside of an airliner, the cockpit," Janet said.

"He is, is he?" Steve asked.

"It seems to me the least you can do is to take the car back to Forest Wood," she added.

"I mean, Steve," Randy said, "after all, turn about is fair play. I let you drive my car, and I'm not even going to hold a grudge about how fast you drove it. And I promise I won't even exceed the speed limit with yours."

Steve tossed him the keys to the convertible.

"Thanks a lot, buddy," Randy said. "Janet and I will be over later. If something doesn't come up, that is."

"Why don't you get him to show you his office at the airport?" Steve said. "That's where he stores all the French perfume."

"I just might do that," Randy said.

"Oh, I couldn't take any perfume," Janet said. She didn't sound at all convincing.

The men from the plant seemed delighted to help Terry and Steve push the Warrior onto the trailer. "I'll buy beer," one of the men said, "if anyone's thirsty."

"Monday, Joe," Terry said firmly. "I have to have a little chat with Mr. Haas."

"Anything you say," Joe said. "It was sure good to see you out here, Mr. Haas, and to know you're interested in racing."

"Likewise," Steve said. "I'll see you all on Monday."

In the pickup truck, even before they'd reached the tunnel from the infield, Steve turned to Terry: "OK, you aged leprechaun, let's hear it."

"Well," Terry began, "It's like this ..."

CHAPTER ELEVEN

ON MONDAY MORNING, at eight-thirty, Steve pushed the button on his intercom and asked Chennowith to come by when he had a free moment. Fifteen minutes later, Chennowith rapped politely at Steve's open door.

"Would you like some coffee?" Steve asked, as he waved him inside.

"No thank you," Chennowith said. "Just had some. What's on your mind?"

"Tell me about the plant sponsoring, or, really *not* sponsoring a race team," Steve said.

"Oh," Chennowith said, and smiled. "I was afraid that would happen."

"Afraid what would happen?"

"That somebody would see you out there, crawling around the line, and bend your ear about it."

"It didn't happen on the line," Steve said. "What was Pickens' objection?"

Chennowith paused a moment before answering. "I suppose you could say that he didn't think the effort and the expense would be worth it." When Steve waited for him to go on, he added, "And it might set a bad precedent."

"I hate to sound like a labor relations expert," Steve said, "because I'm obviously not one, but what about its value in a morale-building sense? Pride in the product, that sort of thing?"

"I suppose Mr. Pickens felt that only a few of the men would be interested, and that the next thing they'd be asking for would be . . . oh, I don't know, a company-sponsored sail plane. . . . or a boat. Or who knows what?"

"And you agree with Mr. Pickens?" he asked.

"I suppose I do. I think it would be more trouble than it was worth. And, then, of course, there would be the danger of embarrassing the company."

"Explain that to me," Steve said.

"The Warrior has an image," Chennowith said, "of being very fast. If the company raced one, and it wasn't fast, then that image would be hurt."

"On the other hand," Steve said, "if the company raced one—and it would really be our local of the union who would race it, not us—and it proved fast on the track, then the company would look good."

Chennowith chuckled. "You sound as if you're in favor of the idea," he said, as if that were out of the question.

"I can't see anything wrong with the idea," Steve said. "I'm going to see Pickens about it."

"Give it some thought, Steve," Chennowith said, "before you commit yourself."

"I have," Steve said, as he got up and walked to the

door. "I'm going to take it up with Pickens, right now."

Pickens doodled on a sheet of notepaper as he heard Steve out. Steve's basic argument was that whatever the cost to the company, it would still be a sound investment in employee relations. Not only would it make the employee feel he was part of a team, but it would give him, Steve said, a feeling of pride in the cars he assembled on the line.

"Maybe," Steve said, trying to make a little joke of it, "it would inspire somebody on the line to make sure the radio knobs were tightened in place."

Pickens looked up at him, and from his face, it was apparent Steve's joke hadn't struck him as at all funny.

"I'll tell you, Haas," Pickens said, "what I told Chennowith. You have discretionary funds in your budget. If you want to use them to build a rocket to fly to the moon, that's your business. Just don't expect me to provide funds from my discretionary budget to buy something you should have bought with yours."

"Mr. Pickens, excuse me," Steve said. "Do I understand you that you didn't veto Mr. Chennowith's idea?"

"I told Chennowith just what I told you," Pickens said, "and left the decision to him."

"I'll see what I can do about getting you a set of owner's credentials for the first race," Steve said.

"Do that," Pickens said drily. "Is there anything else?"

"No, thank you," Steve said, and left. He went back to his office and asked Janet for whatever information she had on the Assembly Line's Discretionary Budget.

She brought him both the *Duties, Authorities and Responsibilities* manual Chennowith had given him the first day in the office, and copies of the ledger sheet showing how the money had been spent for the past two years.

113.45 DISCRETIONARY ALLOWANCE: *The Manager, Assembly Line, will be required to make one-time, and/or unexpected expenditures in the course of his duties. Such expenses may include, but are not limited to, local purchases of hand tools and services; special lighting and/or safety devices; contributions to worker morale and/or welfare activities; unprogrammed travel expenses for himself or other employees (such as participation at industrial conferences); awards made under the Employee Suggestion Program, and other such activities or acquisitions considered in his judgment to be of benefit to the company. An annual allowance of $15,000 is established. The Manager, Assembly Line, will insure that any expenses incurred which may be of a recurring nature will be reflected in his proposed budget for the following year. Requests for expenditures in excess of the prescribed allowance will be forwarded through the General Manager to the office of the Vice President, Fiscal, together with full justification therefor.*

He didn't have to be much of an accountant to read the ledger sheets for the discretionary fund. His predecessor, Claude B. Demmeck, had been miserly with the fund, so far as worker-morale activities had been concerned. The only expenditures under that column had been $15-dollar funeral wreaths to deceased employees or their families. He had bought very few tools or safety devices locally, and awarded a total of $1,100 for employee suggestions for both years. On the other hand, he and Chennowith had managed to spend close to $8,000, about $4,000 a year, attending one conference after another. The first ledger sheet showed that Demmeck had turned back in, at the end of the fiscal year, $8,470.70 as surplus, and $9,109.20 the second year.

There were two ways to view what the ledger sheet showed. The first was that the assembly line was in such perfect running order that it had been unnecessary to buy more than a handful of items to make it run more smoothly; that the employees were either not submitting many suggestions, or if they did, that the suggestions weren't very valuable; and that employee morale was so high and so deeply rooted that it could be maintained by spending a couple of hundred dollars sending funeral wreaths when anyone died. In other words, he could just take the ledger sheet expenditures at face value. The other extreme was that Demmeck and Chennowith had spent whatever they felt like spending while sending themselves to conferences all over the country, but hadn't been willing to part with a dime more for morale and welfare for the employees than was absolutely necessary. He thumbed through the manual again and found another interesting paragraph:

101.50 TRAVEL EXPENSES: *Travel expenses for the Manager, Assembly Line, the management staff, and employees will be funded through the General Manager's Fund. AMC Form 209A will be completed in quadruplicate, with copy Number 1, countersigned by the General Manager, forwarded to Fiscal Division. Copy Number 2 will be made a part of the General Managers' Annual Report. Copy Number 3 will be filed, and Copy Number 4 will be furnished the traveler.*

Steve had a nasty thought: Demmeck and Chennowith had been spending discretionary fund money on their travels. That way, what they spent didn't have to be reported to someone who just might ask where they had gone and why.

It was right on the edge of dishonesty, Steve realized. He also realized that he had a suspicious mind, and that there might be a very good reason for the whole thing.

The answer, he decided, was somewhere between an honest concern for the company's money and an almost brazen scorn for it.

In any event, the manual gave him the authority to spend the money as he saw fit, so long as it was, in his judgment, in the company's interest. As he walked to the canteen for his 9:15 meeting with the men from the assembly line, he had another thought, based on his belief that when people get something for nothing, they really don't appreciate it.

He went to the coffee dispenser and helped himself to a cup of coffee and sat down at a table just as the 9:15 break bell rang.

Less than a minute later, Terry and the men who had been at the race track the day before came into the room, saw him, and sat down at the table while one of the men carried a tray of coffee to the rest.

"Did you see Mr. Pickens?" Terry asked.

"Yeah," Steve said.

"And?"

"The company will do this," Steve said. "We will sell you a car, and whatever parts are needed, at manufacturing cost. We will provide access to the machine shop and plant-vehicle garage, on weekends and at night, at no cost. We will put up 50% of the money for the purchase of the car and parts and racing costs, including insurance and whatever else is required."

"Where are we supposed to get the other 50%?" one of them asked.

"That's your problem," Steve said. "It sounds fair to me."

"And what does the company get out of it?"

"Lettering on the car with the plant name," Steve said. "And half of the profits until it gets its money back."

"And then what?"

"After the loan is repaid, the profits go to the Employee Recreation Fund."

"And what if there are no profits? Then what?" Terry asked.

"Then we split the loss," Steve said. "You don't sound very self-confident."

"He was worse than this in the Army," Terry said. "I used to think he was bucking for general."

"There's one more thing," Steve said. "The company insists on having a member of management as part of the team."

"Oh, great," Terry said. "All we need is some white collar flunky telling us to how to do it. Just who did you have in mind?"

"Me," Steve said, and the others laughed.

"That's worse than I thought," Terry said, smiling broadly. "How soon can we start?"

"As soon as you can go past assembly control, have them make up a computer card," Steve said.

"You mean, old Pickens will actually trust us for the dough?"

"No. Not Mr. Pickens," Steve said. "I will. Mr. Pickens led me to believe that he was giving me enough rope to hang myself. Mr. Pickens was perfectly willing to let me give you the whole thing."

There was a pause at this, and then Terry said thoughtfully, "You didn't have to tell us that, Steve. What was the point?"

"I thought you should know," Steve said. "If this

thing turns out to be a bad idea, I'm the guy who gets it in the neck."

"I thought you management types had the pass-the-buck thing down pat," Terry said.

"Maybe I'll learn how as I go along," Steve replied. "But right now I'm out on the limb."

"Hang on tight," Terry said.

Later that afternoon, Terry came to his office accompanied by Tony Cassilio, the engineer in charge of keeping the line in operation.

"I don't suppose this has anything to do with the operation of the line, does it?" Steve asked.

"Not the way I think you mean," Terry said.

"We·thoug'.t you'd like to see the assembly order before we feed it into the system," Cassilio said.

"How'd you get involved with this, Tony?" Steve asked.

"I'm going to drive it," Cassilio said.

"I thought this was going to be a union project," Steve countered.

"I belonged to the union for a long time before I took over the line," Cassilio said. "I've only been on salary for about a year."

"Besides, he's the only one we know who stands a chance," Terry said.

"If it's OK with the union, it's OK with me," Steve said.

Terry handed him the computer card, and Steve was reminded once again how little he knew of the operation. The little oblong holes in the card, which determined what parts and components would go into it, meant nothing to him. To Tony and Terry, however, each hole meant something. They could read the cards as well, if not as rapidly, as the computer.

"This doesn't do me much good," Steve said. "I'm not that familiar with the card."

"If it's all right with you, Mr. Haas," Cassilio said, "we'll assemble it tonight, on the special order line."

"Suits me," Steve said.

"Janet says she'll not only take care of the paperwork, but set up a set of books for the operation," Terry said. "You want to come watch them put it together?"

"I wouldn't miss it for the world."

At eight-twenty that same night, the metal fingers picked a frame from a vertical stack of them, and Unit 54-71-8945-15 entered the assembly line. It was without question the most stripped model ever to pass down the assembly line.

There was no radio, cigarette lighter or air-conditioning, of course. But there were other parts left off, too. There was no gasoline tank, no seats, no headlights, no headliner or door panels, no outside rearview mirror, no hubcaps and not even handles and locks in the doors.

There was a 437-cubic-inch engine with two four-barrel carburetors, disc brakes, and the largest radiator, wheels, and springs available.

When the car came off the assembly line, it had to be pushed, rather than driven away. With Steve helping, seven men pushed the car to the plant vehicle garage. Steve wasn't at all surprised to find that a service bay just happened to be empty, and that an imposing array of tools just happened to be at that particular bay.

Steve didn't have the heart to ask Terry to show him more of the operation of the line that night; Terry was obviously ready to start building the stripped Warrior hardtop into a racing car. Steve went alone to the line, and stayed there until almost midnight, watching the procedure with which a car was equipped with brakes. For the first time that night, instead of being totally ignored by the workmen on the line, he was given nods of recognition by some men, and some of them actually called him by name.

No matter what else it turned out to be, it was obvious that the news of the company coming up with half the price of a racing car, plus the use of facilities, had spread quickly through the plant grapevine and that the workmen, by and large, were pleased with the idea.

In the morning, there was a neatly typed list of parts and equipment needed for the car lying on his desk. They were going to have to buy a racing seat for the car; a fuel cell; racing tires; a racing helmet for the driver and a long list of other items not available through the company.

Steve called Janet in, and told her to have the purchasing agent buy what was on the list, charging it against his discretionary allowance, and to make sure that the new set of books she had started showed the expenditure of every dime.

"There will be a check, Janet, from the union," he said. "I don't know for how much, but for at least half of what the company's put out so far. Make sure you get a detailed listing of what it cost the company to make that car."

There was to be no check from the union for any money whatever.

Shamefacedly, Terry came to him on Friday, accompanied by five other men and Cassilio.

"I don't know what to say about this, Steve," he said. "But the finance committee turned us down cold. They said the union has no business whatever putting money up for a gamble like this."

"Ouch," Steve said.

"And we can't put the car back on the assembly line, either," Terry said. "We already have the roll bars welded in place, the engine in small pieces for rebuild, the chassis reinforced, and the seat welded in place."

"What do you recommend?"

"We're willing to sign a note at the bank, all of us, and borrow the money."

That solution, Steve realized, would be dandy if they made some money with the car. But if they didn't make any money with the car, if they took it out and wrapped it up badly, they would have to make the note good. That would get around the plant just as quickly as had the news about the car in the first place. The workmen, who seemed to feel that Amalgamated's financial resources were boundless, would be angry about that. On the other hand, if the company put up all the money, not only would it produce the reaction of something-for-nothing's-worth-nothing, but it would be hard to explain to Pickens, not to mention people higher up in the company.

"You guys are sure you want to go through with this?" Steve asked.

"Sure. What else can we do?"

"The company," Steve said even as he made the decision, "will underwrite the cost of everything the company can provide, providing that it has second priority on repayment from winnings."

"Who gets first priority?" Terry asked.

"I can borrow the money for you," Steve said. "For the fuel cell and the rest of the stuff. That will be the first priority of repayment."

"That sounds good," Terry said. "But where are you going to borrow the money?"

"I think I know where to find it," Steve said. "I'll find out for sure over the weekend. Come on in Monday morning, and bring your ball point pen to sign the note."

When they'd gone, he called Janet in and dictated a loan agreement and when she'd typed it up, she brought it back.

"I understand what this says," she said, "but, if you don't mind my saying so, it doesn't say where the cash is coming from."

"That was on purpose," Steve said. "That'll be a secret between you and me. And I mean you alone. Terry's not to know."

He took out his checkbook and wrote a check for $3,500. When it was cashed it would leave him with just over three hundred dollars in the bank.

"I think you're crazy," Janet said, when he handed it to her. "But very nice crazy." And with that, she stood on her tiptoes and kissed him on the cheek.

"Before you get carried away," he said, "and not that I don't like being kissed, I think you should know that was the only answer I could think of. What else could I have done?"

"You could have sold the car for what's in it," she said. "You might even have made a little money on it."

"And how would I—and for that matter, the company—look if I did something like that?"

"You're liable to look a lot worse if Tony takes that car out and wrecks it just as soon as they're finished working on it."

"We'll have to take that chance," Steve said. "Keep your fingers crossed."

CHAPTER TWELVE

STEVE QUICKLY, IF very privately, began to think of himself as Santa Claus, with Terry and the others playing the role of busy little elves. With almost astonishing speed, the car began to take shape.

It proved no trouble at all finding highly skilled workmen in the company to perform individual highly skilled tasks. The array of tools available was a mechanic's dream. The car was lettered, for example, by a workman from the painting division, who had begun work with Amalgamated thirty years before and had spent years as a striper, hand-striping cars in the days long before this could be quickly accomplished with adhesive masking tape. The car was number 15, after the assembly plant's number. The numbers were ornate, lettered in gold, with a black and silver background.

The names of the seven most active members, plus Tony Cassilio's name, were lettered on one door in old English script. NASCAR rules for Grand American Challenge cars forbade the use of slogans on the car, but the Rule Book made no mention of what could be put on the driver's helmet. The painter had drawn a sketch of a leering Indian, above the words "The Wayward Warrior."

The camshaft had been reground by a master tool and die maker, and when Steve saw it before it was put in the engine, it was so finely machined that it looked as if it were chrome plated.

In two weeks, the car was ready. Randy Walsh had, in that time, flown once around the world and made a round-trip to Paris. Steve hoped that Randy's schedule would see him in some far-off exotic place when Number 15 was tested, but Randy arrived home on Friday night, about midnight, and seeing the light in Steve's apartment had come in to announce he wouldn't miss the first test for the world.

Number 15 wasn't going to race that day, but a race was scheduled, and the stands were half-full of dedicated fans even at 8 o'clock, when Number 15 was trailered into the infield.

The car was almost lovingly pushed off the trailer and into the pits. Steve realized that while there was no indication of what kind of racing car it would be, it was certainly the best-looking car at the track.

The NASCAR technical inspection, which took the better part of an hour, turned up no deficiencies, and the inspector volunteered the opinion that it was a craftsmanlike job.

"We wouldn't have this car if it wasn't for you, Steve," Terry said. "So it only seems fair that we give you the first chance to drive it."

Steve gave in to the temptation, refusing to consider the wisdom of driving the car, refusing to consider the unpleasant possibility, and what it would mean, if he wrapped it around a track barrier.

But once he was in the car, he had to admit that he had no right to be there, at least no right to really wring it out and see what it could do. It was the men's car, and they had offered him a ride not because he was a good driver, or because he had money in it (they didn't know he had money in it), but because he was the boss.

He took four laps in the car, and was convinced he hadn't driven it over ninety miles an hour. When he pulled off the course, he was encouraged. It had run smoothly, and there was a really awesome amount of power beneath the hood.

"One oh one point three five zero," Terry said. "That isn't as fast as it would go, is it?"

"It was as fast as it will go with me driving it," Steve replied. "I'm not going to bend it up."

Tony Cassilio got behind the wheel. He had even more trouble crawling in the window than Steve did. He fastened his belt and shoulder straps, adjusted his helmet, and started the engine. Warmed by Steve's laps, the engine sounded smooth and powerful.

Tony burned a little rubber as he let out the clutch in first gear, and he was in high before he reached the end of the pit road. On his third lap around, he shook his left wrist, with its wrist watch, as he passed the pit and his next lap around, he was timed.

His first timed lap was 135.370, and he made better time after that, turning 141.440 and 140.850 in the next two laps. The engine sounded good, a somehow smooth sound despite the roar of the unmuffled exhaust as he swept past them.

Then, entering the first turn on the next lap, the car suddenly reversed direction, swinging its tail to the front as it swerved upward on the banked turn. It made two revolutions, and was starting to make a third when it hit the heavy steel trips of the barrier at the top of the banked curve with its nose. There was a loud crashing noise and the car slowed appreciably. Tony was fighting, without real success, for control. The car slid down the steep curve, and sideswiped the inner track barrier with the left front fender.

Even before he stopped, Steve could hear the whine of the wrecker siren as the wrecker went out. Followed by Terry, he ran down the pit road to the car. Before they got there, Tony had begun to crawl out the window. He was shaken but not apparently hurt.

"Blew a tire," he said, "at the worst possible place."

Number 15 was no longer the prettiest car on the track. The whole front end was shoved in, crushed by the impact against the upper barrier. The left side, which a minute or two before had gleamed with showroom newness was now scraped and bent and torn.

Steve was deeply disappointed, but this, he realized, was no place to show it.

"At least *you're* in one piece," he said. "It can be fixed."

"We're off to a great start," Tony said bitterly, "aren't we?"

"Everybody wraps one up sooner or later," Steve said. "Don't worry about it. We can have it fixed up in time for next week's racing."

"You're really a fountain of optimism, aren't you?" Tony asked.

"With the times you turned," Steve said, with an enthusiasm he didn't really feel, "all we have to do is fix it and get some rubber that'll stand up."

"Maybe we better quit now," Tony said.

"Ah, come on, Tony," Steve said. "One accident isn't the end of it."

When they got back to the pits, Steve saw that the cyclone fence separating the infield from the pits was crowded. He picked out a dozen faces he recognized from the plant. The assemblers were really interested in this car. They couldn't quit now.

Randy Walsh, that night, as they sat at the pool in Forest Wood, watching Janet dive from the board into the water, made it worse.

"I'm one of those unpleasant people who just has to say what he's thinking," he said.

"So say it."

"You sure about this driver of yours? It seems to me he should have been able to steer himself out of that blown tire."

"I suppose you could have?" Steve challenged loyally.

"Yeah," Randy said. "That's what I meant."

"You can't tell what control problems you're going to have with a blowout," Steve said, "and you know it."

"There are some people who have a feeling for driving and some who don't," Randy said. "I don't think Cassilio does. If that makes me a bad guy for saying so, I guess I'm a bad guy."

"I think you're wrong, Randy," Steve said. "Not everybody's blessed with perfection, you know."

"I said it," Randy said, unabashed. "I'm glad I said it, and if I had the chance I'd say it again."

"And I'll say it again," Steve said. "Tony had a little bad luck, that's all."

"I don't suppose it matters, with the Amalgamated bank account behind that car," Randy said. "But I'm glad I don't have any money in it."

On Sunday, they found out the damage to Number 15 was even greater than it had at first appeared. The frame was buckled, and the engine had ripped itself loose from the engine mounts. The radiator was gone, and the left front suspension had been wrecked beyond repair. When they put a chain hoist to the engine to remove it from the chassis, there was a sharp cracking noise and the windshield suddenly splintered into several thousand small pieces. Relieving the pressure of the weight of the engine onto the frame had permitted the twisted frame to press hard enough against the glass to break it.

Steve did some quick figuring with his slide rule and decided it would be cheaper in the long run to strip the original frame and body components of usable and undamaged parts, and to take a new frame and body shell from stock, than it would to try to repair what damage had been done.

Tony Cassilio was very reluctant to enter the car in the races scheduled for two weeks away. He said there wouldn't be time to test the car, even if they could get it finished in time. Steve disagreed. They were going to rebuild it exactly as it had been before; and the only testing they would have to do would be to see that it ran. He'd driven the car, and he trusted his judgment that the design was sound.

There seemed to be a determination on the part of the assembly line workers to get the car running again. Steve went by the plant vehicle garage one night at midnight and found the painter hard at work painting the lettering on the new car. There was a slight change in the new lettering. In small letters, visible only up close, after the 36-inch-high numbers 15 was #2.

Steve went by the garage again on the Friday before they were to race, just to make sure that, during the night shift that followed, the car would be ready.

He found the crew hard at work on the car, and had a sinking feeling in his stomach.

"I hate to sound like the boss," he said. "But you guys are being paid to work on the line, not on the car."

"To tell the truth, Mr. Haas," one of them said. "We hoped you wouldn't find out."

"I'll bet," Steve said, as angry at himself as he was with them.

"What we did was get guys from other shifts to take our places," the man said. "This isn't costing the company any money."

"Well, who's going to take their places on their own shifts?"

"They will. Two, three guys, sometimes four, are just working a couple of hours of our shift, and then they'll do their own shifts."

"That's going to go over great if the union hears about it."

"Don't worry about the union, Mr. Haas."

"Why not? They're going to jump all over me, not you."

"I don't think so," the man said. "We got Lou Feldman on the line, bolting wheels on."

Louis J. Feldman was president of Local 2313, United Automobile Workers of America. Although he had begun work on an assembly line, he had quickly moved up in union ranks, and had been a full time officer of the union for many years.

Steve was so shocked that he said, "I'll have to see that to believe it!"

"Don't do that, Mr. Haas," the man said. "Just let it ride. We're not going to see you in trouble."

"You're going to be finished by tomorrow?"

"We'll be at the track at 8 o'clock in the morning, ready to run it. You going to be able to come out?"

"I'll be there," Steve said.

It wasn't as simple as it sounded. If Lou Feldman, who had gotten into the plant on his union credentials, was hurt in an accident, Employees Compensation wouldn't cover him, because he wasn't an employee, even though he had been and knew how to do the job.

If Pickens saw him on the line, he would recognize him, and there would be trouble. On the other hand, if Steve went to the line, and told him to get off, there would be trouble, not only then, but in the future, with Feldman and others who would not understand his position. The only thing he could do was to keep his fingers crossed and hope that Feldman remembered enough of his skill to keep from hurting himself.

"Listen to me," Steve said, and explained his position to them. They seemed to understand, at least to the point where they agreed that in the future they would not re-arrange their work schedules without his permission. The car had to come second to the efficient operation of the plant, according to the rules.

He left the garage with the feeling he'd often had in the Army, that he had just given the impression that he wasn't a nice guy after all, that beneath a thin veneer, he was all chicken.

That wasn't the reaction he'd hoped he would get from the plant employees.

When he got back to his office, Pickens was waiting for him, and there was something ominous about the questions he asked.

"I just heard about the wrecked car, Mr. Haas," Pickens said. "From the grapevine."

"I suppose I should have told you," Steve admitted. "But it's just about repaired, and it was only a simple accident."

"I suppose that the accident didn't dim any enthusiasm?"

"I'd say it had the opposite effect," Steve said. "They had to build it practically from scratch, and I just found out they're about finished."

"I'm sure you'll see that this interest won't be permitted to interfere with the function of the line," Pickens said.

"I don't think it will, Mr. Pickens," Steve said.

"I don't want it to get out of hand," Pickens said. "In the future, if there is anything as important as an accident, I expect you to tell me about it."

"Yes, sir," Steve said, "I will."

He went to the track the next morning with something less than wild enthusiasm, with an unpleasant feeling that a disaster was about to occur.

Number 15 arrived on a trailer, looking just as pristine as the first # 15 had looked. He wondered if an hour from now, it too would be mangled and battered. If it was wrecked again, he had no money with which to buy parts outside the plant; his $3500 had vanished almost mysteriously, replaced by a thick pad of receipts for expensive components and services.

Cassilio showed up an hour late, and he was anything but confident. Steve was concerned by his attitude, but none of the others seemed to sense it. Feeling at once somewhat foolish and on the other hand, thinking that anything that might help should be used, he kept his left hand in his pocket, fingers crossed, while Cassilio tested the car.

It ran well. Of ten timed practice laps, the slowest speed was 148.740 and the fastest 159.330. It was by no means near the fastest time, but if Cassilio could match that speed in the time trials scheduled to begin at 11, he would not only get himself into the race, but be fairly well up on the starting grid.

And then Cassilio vanished. Everyone presumed that he'd gone for a coke, or something to eat, or was just wandering around the infield. But he didn't show up for the time trials when number fifteen and his name were called.

Steve went to the officials at the starting line and told them they couldn't find their driver.

"Well," the race steward said firmly, "you'd better find somebody with a license to make the time trials, or you're scratched."

Steve returned to the car to find that the others had learned what had happened to Cassilio. He was at the assembly plant. Two electric motors on the engine conveyor line were being replaced for periodic maintenance. Steve had known about it, but it was the sort of thing that happened all the time, and it could easily have been handled by the foreman and men of the Saturday shift. Cassilio didn't have to be there.

"What did he have to go for?" Steve asked impatiently, and then, even as he heard his own voice, he had to ask himself whose side he was on. As the assembly line manager, he could hardly find fault with someone who wanted to do his job.

He found a pay telephone and called the plant.

"Amalgamated Motors, West Point," a determinedly cheerful voice answered.

"Ring the phone in the West Engine Sub-line administrative office," Steve said. "I don't know the number."

"I'm sorry, sir," the operator said, very brightly, "those are restricted telephones and can't be reached."

"This is Mr. Haas, operator," he said. "Put me through."

"I'll connect you with the supervisor, sir," the operator said.

"May I help you, sir?" a new voice inquired.

"This is Mr. Haas. I want to speak to Mr. Cassilio, and he's working somewhere around the West Engine Sub-line."

"I'm sorry, sir," the operator said. "My orders are that we can't connect outside calls to those numbers without permission of the assembly line manager's office."

Steve lost his temper, and was sorry even before he finished saying: "Read your phone book, operator, *I'm* the assembly line manager. Now ring that number."

There was no reply except, in a moment, the buzz of the phone ringing.

"Engine West," a male voice said.

"Mr. Cassilio, please," Steve said. "This is Haas."

"Hang on, I'll get him."

"Yes, Mr. Haas?" Cassilio asked.

"Is there any trouble on the line?" Steve asked.

"No, not really. I'm just watching."

"What about the time trials? Half the plant not on shift is out here waiting to see that car run."

"I thought I'd best be here, Mr. Haas," Cassilio said.

"I'll ask the question again. Is there anything out there your foreman can't handle? Anything out of the ordinary?"

"No. As a matter of fact, the relief motors are just about in place."

"Then you get back out here and race this car," Steve said, and he realized that he sounded far more like a sergeant than an executive.

"You're the boss," Cassilio said.

Steve hung up without saying goodbye, and returned to the car.

"Well, he's on his way," Steve said to Terry. "Let's hope he gets here before the time trials are over."

"Not a chance in the world," Terry said. "Time trials are over in twenty minutes and it's at least that long from the plant. With the traffic outside, it'll even be longer."

"Great," Steve said disgustedly.

"NASCAR rules say you need a licensed driver to make the time trials," Terry said. "They don't say that the same guy who makes the trials has to drive."

"In other words, you think I should make the time trials?"

"What's wrong with that?"

"Well," Steve said, and although he didn't like the idea at all, he could think of only a fairly lame excuse. "What if I bend it up?"

"You won't bend it up," Terry said confidently. "You turned 160 plus driving Randy Walsh's car, and didn't bend that one. Cassilio's only turned 159 tops, and he has wrecked one."

Terry went to the plant pickup truck and took a set of racing coveralls and the elaborately painted helmet from it, and handed them to Steve.

"You're elected," he said. "There's nothing else you can do."

Steve pulled the coveralls over his clothing, and strapped on the helmet. It was a little too tight, and he thought that he couldn't make it all the way through a race with it. But he could wear it for the time trials.

He had a hard time getting into the car. The windows were designed to provide a happy medium between air-flow and wind noise. No engineering consideration had been given to the problem of a man crawling into and out of the car through them.

He adjusted the seat belt, and tightened it, and then pulled the shoulder harness in place. He started the engine and looked out the window for Terry.

Instead he found himself looking at Janet. She smiled at him.

He smiled back, almost laughed, not simply to return Janet's smile, but at himself.

Here I go, he thought, *showing off before a girl. The last time I did something like this, I was twelve years old and rode my bike no hands.*

Then he did laugh out loud. He remembered that the girl's name had been Alma Pelosi, and he had been so intent on not looking at her as he rode the bike that he'd ridden right into the rear of a parked car.

He moved the gear shift lever through its movements, tested the clutch for pressure, dropped it in low and moved out of the pit toward the end of the pit road, where a flagman and an assistant race steward stood.

"Cassilio?" the steward asked when Steve, responding to the flag, stopped.

"No. Haas, S.," Steve said. "Taking the time trial for Cassilio."

The steward ran his finger down a list of drivers and didn't find Steve's name.

"You're not on here, friend," the steward said. "I'll have to see your license."

Getting the license out meant unstrapping himself and then twisting around on the seat, his knees banging against the steering wheel and shaft while he fished his wallet out of the hip pocket of his pants.

"OK," the steward said, after writing his name down. "Take two laps, and we'll time on the third and fourth. Best time gets it."

"I've never driven this car before," Steve said. "How about a couple more practice laps?"

"You should have thought of that before, and taken your practice this morning," the steward said. "If there was time, maybe. But there's no time. Sorry."

"What am I going to have to make to get a position?"

"Somewhere over 162, I'd say," the steward said.

Steve refastened his belts, put the car in gear, and roared onto the track, moving faster than he would have ordinarily, faster than he wanted to. He would have the first lap to get up speed, the second lap for practice, and be timed on the third.

By the time he'd gone into high, he knew that the engine was first rate. The power was quick and sure; he'd burned a little rubber, a chirp, going into high, and he realized he must have been doing close to eighty when he went into high.

Coming down the start/finish straightaway completing the first lap, he wound it up. Just before he lessened pressure on the accelerator to slow for the first turn, he dropped his eyes to the tachometer. The needle was beyond 6,000 and there had been no suggestion of the hesitation that meant valve float. From the centrifugal pressure on his seat as he went around the first turn, he knew he was moving.

He was beginning to feel a little confidence now. If he had turned 160 something in Randy's car, he would do better in this one. He might be able to move Cassilio up pretty far on the starting grid, perhaps far enough so that Cassilio, running a safe and sane race, might even place in the top ten.

Going down the rear straightaway, he ran it as fast as it would go. The tachometer fluttered around 6,500 rpm, too fast, really, for he knew that he was right on the edge going around the second turn. He sensed the loss of adhesion on all four wheels.

When he passed the starting-line this time, the watches would be started, and he would be timed. The car was handling beautifully, although already his arms and wrists were beginning to feel tingly, as if they were asleep, from the vibration passing through the suspension and steering systems to the wheel.

He regretted not wearing gloves. But he had none here, and his hands were much larger than Tony's, and he hadn't even tried to pull Tony's gloves on.

Before he slowed for the first turn again, he dropped his eyes to the tachometer. The needle was down around 5,700. He felt confident that he could run it around 6,000, maybe a shade over that. Coming out of the turn, he pressed hard on the accelerator, and kept his eyes off the tach. He would drive it somewhere between what he felt was fast and what the seat of his pants told him was foolish.

He seemed to have, by luck, found the groove coming out of the first turn. When he applied pressure to the accelerator, the forward movement was swift and sure, no fishtail, no movement but straight ahead.

He was moving so fast that he had to go wide on the second turn to retain control, but then there seemed to be another groove, and he came out of it fast, moving at a shallow angle across the track from the outer edge to the inner, passing the start/finish line close to the inner side.

Well, he thought, as he eased up on the accelerator, that was the best he could do. If he didn't get Cassilio a spot, no one could say that he hadn't tried. Nobody could blame him if Cassilio couldn't start because of his times. Cassilio should be driving, not him.

By the time he'd gone through the first turn, the rear straightaway and the second turn, he was moving relatively slowly, about 85 or 90 miles per hour. He touched the brakes, felt himself thrust against the shoulder harness and then touched them again, entering the pit road at 60. He put the shift lever into second and let out the clutch. The engine roared, and then he braked a final time and shut off the engine.

Terry came to the car, and Steve handed him the helmet. His head hurt.

"How'd I do?" Steve asked.

"My watch didn't work," Terry said, then, "Wait a minute. Here's the announcement."

Steve pushed his head out the window to listen to the public address system. He only caught the tail end of the message. "—one point one ninety-one off the track record set by Tiny Lund in 1970," the announcer said.

Steve looked at Terry in confusion.

Terry said, "So the watch was right. One seventy-nine point two eighty-five. It looks to me like we hired the wrong driver."

# CHAPTER THIRTEEN

IN THE MIDST of every raincloud, Steve told himself the next morning, there is at least one ray of sunlight. In this particular rainstorm, however, he had to search hard to find a couple of dim glimmers.

For one thing, he told himself, Randy was scheduled for a lengthy flight and wouldn't be around for two weeks. That meant that after they drove him to the airport, following brunch with Janet and Margaret, Terry's girl, Steve would more or less have Janet to himself for the next fourteen days, while Randy was off in faraway places.

For the second glimmer, he thought it was highly unlikely that Mr. Pickens would read the Motor Racing Sports section of the *Atlanta Chronicle,* or that, if he did happen to be checking golf, baseball, or other scores, his eye would fall on a paragraph far down in the story in which Steve's name was mentioned.

Out in the 87th lap with undisclosed engine trouble was Tony Cassilio, running 28th at the time. His car, a Mohawk Warrior, had earlier in the time trials with S. Haas at the wheel, turned a surprising 179.285, 1.191 off Tiny Lund's track record. Cassilio, an engineer, is with the Mohawk assembly plant in West Point, and his car is a joint factory-employee entry.

If, by chance, Pickens did read the story, there were a number of things in it which would not please him. For one thing, Steve felt sure that Pickens would object to him driving the car as being beneath the dignity of the management team. More importantly, Number 15 was not a joint factory-employee entry. It was an employee entry, period. The Mohawk Division of the Amalgamated Motors Company had a racing team, and the brass would not at all like to think that one of the assembly plants was running competition to it, even if—or maybe especially because—that entry had been running 28th in a field of 29 when engine trouble forced it out of the race.

That engine trouble was mysterious, too. Cassilio had just pulled into the pits and announced the car was running roughly, and that he'd lost engine pressure. The engine had sounded all right to Steve, and when he'd checked the pressure, he was getting better than 60 pounds per square inch.

That left two possibilities, both of them unpleasant. First, that Tony was telling the truth and something *was* wrong with the engine which was causing intermittent loss of oil pressure and roughness. The second possibility was that Tony wasn't telling the truth, and that he had come in because the racing had been too much for him. He didn't like to consider the possibility that Tony was a liar, or what they would do if Tony found another excuse not to run.

Taking the time trials himself had been a major mistake, but there was nothing much he could do about it except take whatever pleasure he could from Glimmers #1 and #2. He would have some time with Janet, and Pickens probably wouldn't read the paper.

Glimmer #1 grew even dimmer when they drove Randy to the airport. Janet insisted on sticking around and watching Randy's plane take off. Steve didn't think he had an overdeveloped inferiority complex. He thought he was just being realistic to understand that someone who was a co-pilot of something as large as a Boeing 747 had an appeal for the fair sex that he couldn't match, either as an old buddy of the lady's brother, or as manager of the assembly line.

He kept his fingers crossed literally and figuratively on Monday when he went to work. By Wednesday, he had begun to relax a little. Mr. Pickens had indeed brought up the subject of Number 15, but it hadn't been at all bad.

"I understand, from what I've heard in the plant, that Mr. Cassilio had something less than an unqualified success at the racetrack?" Pickens had asked, making it a statement.

"He placed 28th in a field of 29, Mr. Pickens," Steve said.

"Well," Pickens said, and he smiled. "I suppose someone has to lose, you know."

"I'm sure he'll do better," Steve said.

"The men seem to be very interested," Pickens said. "Maybe it's a good thing after all."

Steve just nodded and smiled.

On Thursday, things got worse. He went to the plant vehicle garage early in the morning to learn

what they'd found out about the intermittent roughness and loss of oil pressure in the engine of Number
15.

"There's nothing we can find wrong with it," Terry
told him. "We've decided it must have been a faulty
oil pressure gauge, so we replaced it." From the tone
of his voice, Steve could tell that Terry shared his
suspicions about Tony being unwilling to race, and
immediately, Terry confirmed this.

"We've been talking, Steve," he said. "And, well,
you just can't argue with results, and you did turn
almost 180—

"I don't think I want to hear the rest of this."

"We were thinking that maybe we ought to suggest tactfully to Tony Cassilio that he step down—"

"That's entirely up to you," Steve said. "But while
you're still talking, you'd better consider who else
you'd get to drive it. I'm not going to drive it."

Terry looked at him, and the smile vanished for a
moment, than came back on, and he said: "Whatever
you say, boss."

"I can't drive, Terry," he said. "It's as simple as
that. It would get me in trouble with the company."

"Why?"

"Among other things, the company already has a
racing team," Steve said. "So long as this is an employee car, fine, but it gets awkward the minute it
looks as if the factory is sponsoring it."

"Well, like the man said, if you don't really want to
do something, one excuse is as good as another."

"It's not that I don't want to," Steve said.

"I heard you the first time," Terry said. "But you
will be at the races?"

"Yes, I will," Steve said. "In the seats. As a paying
spectator, in the company of your sister."

"I don't suppose you'd want to loan me your helmet, would you?" Terry asked. "I want to run this car

myself. Not for speed, but just to convince myself that . . . of something. I can't get into Tony's. And no cracks about a big head, please."

"You can have my helmet," Steve said. "I'll bring it to work in the morning."

On Saturday, Steve went to the plant and tried to make serious inroads into the mountains of paperwork that Chennowith lately had been routing over his desk. Some of the decisions called for were minor, the sort of thing that a line foreman, or a middle-manager, or certainly Chennowith should have made by himself. They didn't have to ask Steve for permission to have air-driven tools sent off for overhaul, for example, or whether or not he thought it was time to repaint safety line markers.

He made a short note to himself on his desk pad: "Get Chennowith to stop sending me all his junk," so that he could take care of it first thing in the morning on Monday.

Then he drove to his apartment, and substituted his glen plaid suit for a yellow knit shirt and light blue pants, and his highly shined wingtips for a pair of rubber soled, suede ankle-high boots. He went downstairs, put the top down on his car, put the top cover boot in place with the irreverent thought that as long as they had been making convertibles, they still hadn't come up with a better way to do it than the grunt, stretch and sweat method, and went to pick up Janet.

He wasn't really surprised to see familiar faces from the plant in the grandstands, but he was surprised to see them in the expensive seats. While there was no question that the highly skilled employees were making enough money to pay for whatever seats they wanted, the fact that they had bought the best available seemed to prove again that they were really interested in how "their" car was doing.

He watched Number 15 move out of the pits toward the track and relaxed a little. Cassilio had shown up, apparently, and Steve was able to put away the troublesome idea that he was running scared, and wouldn't show up.

"Car Number 15," the public address system said. "A Mohawk Warrior driven by Tony Cassilio. Cassilio placed 28th at the Atlanta 300 last week."

Janet looked at him and smiled and waved her crossed fingers at him.

"He'll do all right," Steve said, with a good deal more confidence than he really felt.

Tony did not do all right. For the first two laps, it looked as if he had never driven a car at that kind of speed before. He was all over the track, smoke showing at the tires on curves, going either too fast or too slow. It would be a miracle, Steve decided, if he qualified.

And then, as if there was some kind of major effort on Tony's part, there was one lap which, if it couldn't honestly be called good, was at least passable. He smoked on the turns, losing both speed and control, but made it up with a tremendous burst of speed on the rear straightaway, going so fast that Steve thought his getting around the second turn was far more luck than driving skill.

"Cassilio, in Number 15, best of two timed laps," the public address system announced, "turning 159.-005."

"That's not very good, is it?" Janet asked.

"Well," Steve said, "he'll get better."

And then, in the grandstands in front of him, Steve saw one of the men who made up the crew, obviously looking desperately for someone in the stands. When he saw Steve, his face visibly relaxed and he came running up the concrete steps of the aisle.

"I got to see you, Mr. Haas," he said.

"After the race," Steve said. "I'm here to watch."

"It can't wait until after the race," the man said.

"Tony'll do all right," Steve said. "Just relax."

"The bum didn't show up at all," the man said.

"Then who was that?" Steve asked.

"Terry," the man said.

"He doesn't know how to drive a car like that," Steve said, thinking aloud, and adding, "and he doesn't have a license."

"That's what we told him," the man said. "But you can't argue with Terry when he gets an idea."

"I can argue with him," Steve said, and Janet parroted that: "Well, I can argue with him. He's going to kill himself."

In a straight line, in other words, across the track from where they sat, they were no more than 100 yards from Terry Fallon and Warrior # 15. But going around, out of the grandstands, along the back of the grandstands, through the pedestrian tunnel, and then to the infield, past the pit gate, and to the car took some time. Steve and Janet ran, and she took his hand, to keep from getting separated, and he reflected that it was the first time she'd held his hand.

"What are you up to, you maniac?" Steve demanded when he finally reached Terry.

"Not bad, huh?" Terry said. "For my first time out. 159.005."

"You're going to kill yourself," Steve said.

"Why should I? That's almost as fast as Cassilio, that unmentionable, ever went. And he had practice."

"You're not going to race, and that's it," Steve said. "I'll blow the whistle on you with the track steward, Terry, I promise I will."

"Look, there's three, maybe four hundred guys from the plant out there, most of them with their families. They paid a lot of dough to watch this car run, and I have just found out that I can run it."

"You can like hell," Steve said. "You were all over the track. You'd kill yourself, and probably half a dozen other people. You're out of your mind, that's what you are."

"Well," Terry said triumphantly, "there is one way out of this little problem."

"Not on your life," Steve said, immediately understanding him.

"I'll level with you," Tony said. "What I was going to do was learn how to drive this thing, get you to teach me. Honest to God, Steve, I had no idea that miserable Cassilio wouldn't show up. I thought he would show up, and do miserably, and then I could start driving it. But he didn't. He didn't even send word. He just chickened out, period."

"I'll teach you drive it," Steve said. "But there's hardly time to do that now. The race starts in fifteen minutes."

"So what it boils down to is that either I drive it, or you drive it."

"You won't drive it," Terry said. "I'll tell the steward you don't have a license. I'll tell him you took that time trial without a license. I mean it, buddy, and you know I do."

"If you did that," Terry said, "the car would be suspended for racing for 180 days. You know the Rule Book as well as I do."

"OK. So I don't tell the steward. But that also means you don't drive it."

"We're right back where we started from," Terry said. "You're elected, by a process of elimination."

"No," Steve said flatly.

"Look, be reasonable. You know you can drive it. All you have to do is go around and around out there in a long left turn. I'm not saying you should go out there and win it. Just go out there and let the people from the plant see their car running. Then we get a

little bit of money back, as much as a thousand dollars
if you can finish the race without losing oil pressure."

"No," Steve repeated.

"Well, then, wish me luck."

"I'll tell the steward," Steve repeated.

"That'll make you the most popular guy in the
plant, won't it?" Terry challenged. "Come on, sarge,
be reasonable."

"Give me my hard hat, you miserable—" Steve
said, biting off the rest of it with a massive effort.
"And get out of that racing suit."

Terry smiled at him, a smug, self-satisfied smile
that came a good deal closer to earning him a fistful
of knuckles than he could possibly have imagined.

"Driver's meeting at the center of the pits," the
public address system announced. "All drivers report
to the driver's meeting."

Steve Haas was the last driver to show up, and the
steward didn't like it.

"You're late, mister," he said. "How come?"

"Last minute change of drivers," Steve said.
"Something came up." That, he decided, was the
understatement of the year.

There was nothing spectacular in the driver's
meeting, just the usual last minute instructions, and
the inevitable plea for the drivers to keep their eyes
out for caution flags.

When the meeting broke up, Steve didn't have to
walk far to the car. There were 36 starters, and he
was number 34, and the starting lineup stretched
from the start/finish line back almost to where the
meeting had been held.

He crawled into the car and adjusted the straps.
He ran his eyes over the gauges, and tested the gear
shift throw and the clutch pressure. Then he looked
out at Terry.

"Don't think this is the end of this," he said. "I'm not finished with you yet, you self-satisfied idiot."

"That's it, boy, we need that fighting spirit."

Steve realized that if he hadn't been strapped in, he really would have thrown a punch at Terry.

"Gentlemen," the public address system boomed, "start your engines."

The roar was incredible. He realized, too late, that he had done nothing to protect his ears from the roar. He motioned Terry back to the window.

"Rip me off a piece of your shirt," Steve ordered, and Terry saw that he wasn't kidding. He pulled his shirt tail from his pants and ripped off a foot square piece of it.

"In two," Steve shouted, and Terry complied.

Steve had time, before the flag went down, to work a folded piece of Terry's shirt over his right ear. Then they were moving around the track, following the pace car. With one hand, Steve folded the other piece of shirt into a pad and forced it under the helmet. It was some help, but it wasn't going to give the protection it should.

He was into the first turn now, with the front running cars stretched out quarter-way down the backstretch. They were picking up speed, but they were by no means at starting speed.

There was no start the first time around, but on the second lap, the steward in the open pace car held his finger up in the air. One more lap, then the next time around, the race—presuming the cars were maintaining a good starting position—would begin.

Steve was just about to enter the start-finish straightaway when, far ahead, he saw the green starting flag flash downward. The cars in front immediately began to accelerate. The rules required that the cars actually cross the starting line in the position they'd earned on the starting grid. This meant that while the cars in the rear would accelerate, they couldn't accelerate to the point where they would pass anyone ahead of them until they were across the line.

It didn't matter, Steve told himself, because he had no intention of trying to win this thing for the very good reason that he stood no chance to win it. He was just going to run a nice, fast race and stay out of trouble. If Mr. Pickens hadn't seen that Cassilio had placed 28th of 29 entries, it was unlikely he would notice S. Haas had placed 36th in a field of 36.

This was not to say that Steve was going to throw the race. As soon as the flagman passed him on the right, he put his foot to the floor and Number 15's engine roared, the acceleration pressing him against the thin cushions of the seat.

He was outside, and he moved farther outside, gaining speed in high, and going around three or four cars before he was halfway through the first turn. He knew enough about racing to get away from the tail end of the pack; accidents happened when the front runners began to lap the tail of the pack at early stages of the race. He wanted to be just by himself on the track when the front runners went around him.

The front runners were already far ahead of him, and when he turned onto the rear straightaway, it was clear. He shoved harder on the accelerator and dropped his eyes to the tachometer. He was doing over 6200 when he slowed for the second turn.

And then, ahead of him on the track, he saw the pile-up, cars still moving sideways, one of them rolled over. If he slowed now, lost the torque on his wheels, he would likely lose the car. He put it onto a four-wheel drift, sideways, to lose speed, and headed for the inside of the track, straightening at the last moment to whip past a flagman furiously waving a yellow caution flag, and then slowing on the straightaway to take up position behind the car ahead of him.

As he passed the far end of the pit road, he saw the pace car waiting its turn to get on the track. He had a long time to wonder about what had happened, and to consider the odd fact that somehow he'd moved up from 34th to 18th. That was simple to determine by just counting the cars ahead of him in the dutiful line following the pace car.

There had been a major wrap-up coming out of the second turn, and it had taken at least six, and possibly eight cars out of the race. The caution flag stayed up for fifteen laps while track workmen frantically removed the wrecked cars, and the debris from them, and spread an absorbent material on the track to soak up the spilled oil and water.

Then, far ahead of him, he saw that the steward in the pace car was holding his finger aloft, and that the flagman was waving the white flag. The next time around, the race would be restarted.

This time the cars were bunched on the start/finish straightaway when the green flag came down. Steve was inside now, beside a red Chevrolet Camaro. The blue Mercury Cougar ahead of him moved out quickly, and Steve followed on his tail, moving to the outside when he was past the Camaro. He rode the rail outside through the first turn, gaining speed through the turn, and stayed outside on the rear straightaway, only dimly aware that he was passing a good many cars.

Coming out of the second turn, he saw that four cars were bunched ahead of him, and that the Cougar he'd passed before was right on his tail. He had a feeling of exhilaration, almost of madness. There seemed to be no limit to the power he had under his foot. By the time he was through the second turn, he

had closed the distance between him and the four
cars in front, and was running outside in fifth place.

On the front straightaway, he decided he would
have nothing to lose by trying to get around, and that
taking at least one lap would be a good thing. He
rode outside, three car widths from the rail, and
passed the cars in third and fourth place before slowing for the turn. He was forced back to fourth going
through the first turn, but the wild idea bore fruit on
the rear straightaway. He let himself drift outside,
and then held his foot to the floor. There was a moment's terror near the point where he would have to
slow for the second turn, a moment when it appeared the car in lead place would not give way.

But then it did, and on the edge of losing control
Steve entered the first turn in first place. When he
came out of it, on the rear straightaway, he increased
his lead, and saw in the mirror that the Mercury was
still on his tail.

He talked to himself, telling himself that what he
had done was both grandstanding and not at all
unusual. He was not the first driver to take chances
like that, and most of the top racers really didn't
mind; hotshots had a way of either spinning out or
blowing up after a spectacular burst of speed.

But on the other hand, there was an undeniable
thrill in knowing that he was out in front, and he
decided he would just stay there and see what happened. The car seemed to be running superbly, and
there was no reason to slack off now.

He stayed out in front for sixteen laps, with the
Mercury riding behind him, taking advantage of his
draft, which permitted him to run just as fast with
much less strain and fuel consumption than Steve, a
gift of the law of aerodynamics to racing drivers.

On the 43rd lap, the Old Driver's Tale came true.
Steve had just applied pedal pressure to come out of

the second turn when the engine came apart. First there was a high, piercing shriek, the sound of metal on metal, and then, a fraction of a second later, a sound under the floorboards like hail on a tin roof. He just had time to consider that his transmission had come apart, and that the noise he had heard was the pieces hitting the safety shield when there was a third, far more ominous sound, a dull whooshing thump, and then flames coming out of wheel wells, orange and blue, flashing around the windshield.

He was out of control now, moving sideways, nose pointed to the outside of the track. He threw the shift lever into second before he remembered that he no longer had a transmission. When he put his foot to the brake, he felt a vile taste in his mouth as he thought he had lost brakes too.

But then there was a slowing sensation, and he snapped the wheel hard to the left, and the car straightened and rode parallel to the retaining wall, still slipping sideways. He hit the retaining wall flat, and it bounced him off, and spun him around, and when the flames were blown aside for a second, he saw the strands revolve crazily around him as he spun, and for a moment, he saw cars coming down the track toward him, and then in another fleeting instant, as he jerked the wheel, he saw the pit retaining wall and hoped he wasn't going to hit that.

He stabbed the brakes again to try to regain control, aware that he'd taken away much of their life already, hitting them at 160 or whatever he was doing coming out of the turn. But there was enough left in them to give him control, and out the side window he could see that he was running parallel to the pits.

He could see nothing straight ahead, that was all flames, and he realized that he was breathing smoke now, and fumes, and held his breath. He snapped the wheel to the right and went into a drift, and then straightened again. The more speed he lost the greater the flames seemed to be. He snapped the wheel to the right, and jammed his brake foot to the floor. There was a suggestion that the car was going to turn over, and then there was nothing under the brake pedal at all. He tried to correct to the right, and then there was a horrible sound of rending metal as he ran into the pit retaining wall.

Then, incredibly, he saw that he was stopped. The flames were coming into the passenger compartment now, and he wanted desperately to take a breath but didn't dare to. He unfastened the seat and shoulder harness and threw himself through the window, pawing his way out, feeling a sudden warmth on his leg. He fell to the ground and crawled away from the car. Then he tried to get to his feet to run, and his right leg buckled under him. He crawled with his elbows and his left leg, and then someone was holding his shoulders, and dragging him, at a fast pace.

Then they stopped dragging him, and he looked around and saw the concrete blocks of the pit retaining wall. They were saying something to him, but he had no idea what it was. He rolled over and held himself up on his elbows.

Number 15 was completely in flames, and then, as half a dozen men sprayed thick white columns of carbon dioxide on it, the flames were snuffed out, and it just sat there, smoldering, looking as if somehow, miraculously, snow had fallen on it, that summer day.

He looked down at his leg, where he'd felt the warmth, thinking the gasoline fire had burned him. The leg wasn't burned. It was bloody. He was bleeding, and just before he passed out, he saw a man rip the pants of the one-hundred-dollar, fire-resistant suit to get at his leg.

CHAPTER FOURTEEN

STEVE WOKE UP once in the ambulance, passed out again, and then he woke up again in the emergency room at the hospital.

"Ouch," he said to the doctor working on his leg.

"You stayed out just long enough," the doctor said. "I'm finished."

Steve sat halfway up and looked down at his leg. There was a row of neat black sutures in his calf.

"Is that all that happened?"

"Well, you don't have any eyelashes or eyebrows, but, yes, I'd say the greatest damage was to your leg."

"That's what you think," Steve said.

"I beg your pardon?"

"I'm going to have a hard time explaining this to my boss."

"Your boss ought to be glad you're alive," the doctor said. "I saw what happened. I would have given good odds you'd be a customer for a casket, rather than just a few neat little stitches."

"Where am I, at the track?"

"No, you're in Southern General Hospital," the doctor said.

"How'd you see the accident, then?"

"It was on television."

"Oh, great," Steve said. "Great."

"You feel all right?"

"Ginger-peachy, thank you," Steve said.

"Well, I'm going to give you a shot, and let you get a good night's sleep. I suppose you've used up today's supply of energy, as well as adrenalin, anyway."

"I don't want a shot," Steve said. "I have to do some serious thinking."

"A little prayer of gratitude might be in order," the doctor said, "and I didn't ask you if you wanted a shot, I told you you're getting one."

He woke up the next time to the sound of a telephone ringing. He was in a large and sunny hospital room which smelled like a florist's place of business. Or, he thought, staring angrily at the telephone, like a funeral home.

Finally, he reached for the phone and barked hello into it, sure that it was a wrong number.

"Steve?" his mother's voice asked. "Are you all right?"

"Just fine, Mom, just fine," he said.

"We saw it on television, Harry and I, but we didn't know it was you until they called from the plant. Mr. Hickens, or something. Nice man."

"Pickens, Mom," Steve said. "Mr. Pickens."

"He said there was nothing for me to worry about, that you're going to be all right."

"Just fine, Mom, just fine," he said again.

"Harry wants to talk to you," she said, and his mother's husband came on the line.

"You're all right, Steve? Anything we can do? You want us to come down there?"

"No," Steve said. "Thank you. All I had was a couple of stitches."

"Boy, that was a wreck," Harry volunteered. "I'm glad your mother didn't know it was you."

"Me, too."

"I didn't know the company had you driving race cars," Harry said. "I suppose you didn't want to worry your mother?"

"Something like that, Harry," Steve said.

"Here's your mother again," he said, and they spoke again for a minute or two, and then said goodbye.

Fifteen minutes later, there was a gentle knock at the door.

"Come in," Steve said.

It was Terry and Janet, and, of all people, Randy Walsh.

"I thought you were in Arabia or someplace," Steve said.

"You know how the airline business is," Randy said. "You never know. Boy, it really got your face, didn't it?"

"I don't know," Steve said, and put his hands to his face. It felt like he had whiskers where his eyebrows had been. Directly at the foot of the bed was the washstand. He sat up and examined himself in the mirror above it. His hair was mussed, and he was absolutely bare of facial hair, except for the growth of stubble of his beard. Here and there he was daubed with what appeared to be either merthiolate or mercurochrome, or little dabs of grease, apparently for burns.

He could not help making the comparison between Haas, in the backless hospital gown in which someone had dressed him, looking like he'd just come home from the wars, and Randy Walsh, handsome, blond, in full possession of his facial hair and wearing a very elegant suit. Then Randy put the final grain of salt in the open wound. He put his arm around Janet, and she obviously liked it, snuggling closer, and said,

"Well, Janet and I wanted to come see you, but maybe you'd rather not have any visitors."

"Thank you for coming," Steve said, and forced a smile. They left, but Terry remained behind. All the time Janet had been in the room, Steve had been rehearsing in his mind exactly what he would say the moment Janet was gone, so that her maidenly ears wouldn't be burned by it.

But he couldn't even do that. Terry looked so down in the mouth that he didn't have the heart to tell him off.

"Oh, relax, Terry," Steve said finally. "You didn't force me into that car with a gun. It really was my own fool idea."

"Gee," Terry said. "You look awful."

"It's always nice to have your friends cheer you up," Steve said.

"I promised the guys, Steve, that I'd call them just as soon as I got to see you," Terry said.

"Get out of here, before I throw something at you," Steve said. Terry waved and left, and then immediately reappeared, carrying the Sunday paper.

"I bought this for you," he said. "I bought six copies, as a matter of fact."

"Explain that," Steve said.

Terry walked to the bed and handed him the thick paper. "You're just about all over the front page of the sports section," he said, and then he fled.

Steve found the sports section. There was a five-column picture of Number 15 sliding sideways past the pits, apparently completely engulfed in flames. Steve offered the little prayer of thanksgiving that the doctor had suggested the day before.

The story was going to go over great in the paneled offices at Amalgamated, Detroit: It had his name spelled correctly, and the reporter had been diligent enough to report that not only was he an Amalgamated employee, but the manager of the assembly line at West Point, Georgia's Assembly Plant Number 15.

Steve was not allowed to wallow in self-pity for long, however, about either his trouble with the company, or with his injury. Hungry, he pushed the call button.

"Something wrong?" the nurse, a middle-aged woman, asked.

"I'm hungry. Can I get something to eat?"

"You're ambulatory," she said, matter of factly. "You'll find a bathrobe in the closet, and the cafeteria down the hall. Just sign the check. They'll put it on your bill."

"If I'm ambulatory, that means I can leave?"

"We don't discharge patients on Sunday," she said. "You'll have to wait until after you see the doctor in the morning."

After he had something to eat, the same nurse told him that she was sorry, but that all the television rental sets had been rented.

Monday morning, at quarter to ten, Janet reappeared, alone.

"How do you feel?"

"As soon as I see the doctor, who has been expected momentarily since seven," Steve said, "I can go. Presuming someone'll get some clothes for me from my apartment."

"Randy thought you'd be needing some clothes," she said. "He told me he'd bring a suit for you."

"That was nice of him," Steve said, and he realized he sounded a little sarcastic.

"I thought it was," she said. "He's really a very nice guy."

"And you're just a little stuck on him, huh?"

"More than a little," she said.

"That figures," Steve said. "Are congratulations in order?"

"Not quite yet," she said. "But don't put them where you can't find them in a hurry." She said that with a smile, and then she added, "Mr. Pickens said that I'm to do whatever I can to make you more comfortable, and that you shouldn't worry about coming in to work." Then the smile was gone. "He also said that he thought you'd like to see this." She handed him a company Telex message.

FROM VICE PRESIDENT ADMINISTRATION DETROIT
TO GENERAL MANAGER ASSEMBLY PLANT 15

AS SOON AS PRACTICAL CONSIDERING HIS PHYSI-
CAL CONDITION, PLEASE ARRANGE FOR MR STEFAN
HAAS TO COME TO DETROIT FOR CONSULTATIONS.

JEROME B. TORNELL

"Well, I can't say I didn't expect it," Steve said.

"Steve," Janet said. "Terry got you into this, didn't he?"

The obvious answer to that was you bet your last nickel he did, and Steve almost said just that. But then he realized that it wasn't true, that he was in trouble, indeed, in the hospital, because of a guy named Steve Haas and nobody else.

"No, not at all," he said.

"I don't believe that," she said. "You're a nice guy, Steve, for saying it."

"Number Two always tries harder," he said. "Don't you know that?"

She smiled at him, warmly, even, but at the same time the smile told him that he stood little chance of moving up to Number One.

"Is there anything you want me to tell Mr. Pickens? He'd said he'd come by to see you after work."

"Do me a favor, Janet," Steve said. "Wait until about four o'clock and then tell Mr. Pickens thanks for wanting to come, but I'm on my way to Detroit."

"You don't have to do that, Steve," Janet said. "Wait till you feel better."

"That's like giving the condemned man a rest cure before hanging him," he said. "Will you do what I ask?"

"Sure," she said. "I owe you, anyway."

"For the Boy Bird Man?"

"I wouldn't have met him, except for you."

"Invite me to the wedding," he said.

"We will, of course," she said.

At five past one, Stefan B. Haas, Assembly Line Manager, Plant Number 15, Category 20, pushed open the door of the Atlanta Transportation Office of the Amalgamated Motors Corporation and walked to the receptionist's desk to arrange transportation to Detroit.

"Oh," the blonde from the Dallas Transportation Office said, "Mr. Haas, how nice to see you again." Then, in shock, "What happened to your eyebrows?"

"Like the moth," Steve said. "I got too close to the flame."

"What are you doing here in Atlanta?"

"I work here," Steve said, and wondered if he should have phrased it in the past tense. "I used to work here."

"So do I," she said. "I was transferred just a week ago."

"That's good," Steve said. "Are you happy?"

"Well, I don't know anyone at all here, hardly," she said, and Steve recognized that for a cue. It seemed a little bit late for that, but there was no sense hurting her feelings by letting her think he wasn't interested.

"The very next time I get to town, I'll introduce you to a bachelor," he said.

"Who?"

"Me."

"How interesting," she said. "I'll look forward to it."

She gave him a first class ticket on a Delta flight leaving in thirty minutes, and during the half hour in which he had a chance to talk to her, and on the flight to Detroit, he thought that really put the final nail in his coffin. If he hadn't gotten into this trouble, he certainly would have traveled, and he certainly would have met her in the office. The way it had turned out, meeting her this time was even worse than the first time. Then, at least, he could look forward to passing through Dallas again on company business. He didn't expect to be on the company payroll long after he arrived in Detroit.

He didn't even have the heart to go back to the D'Arcy Arms Residential Hotel. He checked into the airport motel, and then took a cab out to the Amalgamated Administration Building.

The secretary in Tornell's outer office raised her eyebrows at Steve's appearance, but restrained herself from comment. Tornell didn't.

"Well, if it isn't the speed demon of the raceways," he said. "What happened to your eyebrows?"

"Let's get this over with," Steve said, none too politely.

"Well, we really didn't expect you so soon, after we

heard you were in the hospital," Tornell said. "But with your reputation, I suppose I should have known better."

Steve decided that a nasty crack would serve no purpose whatever, so he said nothing.

Tornell pushed the button on his intercom. "Mr. Barrens, Jerry Tornell."

"Go ahead, Jerry."

"Haas is in my office."

"So soon? I thought he was in the hospital?"

"He's here. When would it be convenient for you to meet with us, Mr. Barrens?"

"Right now," the voice of the Vice President, Administration, said. "We might as well get it over with as soon as possible."

"We'll be right there, sir," Tornell said, and stood up as he switched off the intercom. Steve followed him down a corridor and into a large outer office. The secretary there said, "Mr. Barrens expects you, gentlemen, go right in, please."

Barrens didn't react as Steve expected him to.

"My God, Haas," he said, "what happened to your eyebrows?"

"I had a—an auto accident."

"I daresay you did," Barrens said. "It was on front pages all over the country. You're lucky you're alive."

"Yes, sir, I know."

"You sure you're all right?"

"Yes, sir," Steve said. "I feel fine." That wasn't quite the truth, but it was true of his physical condition, if not his mental condition.

"I always hate these things," Barrens said, as he waved them into chairs. "This is the part of the business I really don't like."

Steve wondered if that was his cue to offer his resignation. For some reason he was hesitant to do so;

he decided to wait. Possibly he would get off with what in the Army had been called a first class chewing out.

Barrens tapped a folder on his desk, a personnel record. "This represents many years of a man's life," he said. "Many of them representing devotion to duty and absolute truthworthiness."

Steve had the odd idea that he wasn't being discussed. Three years could hardly be called "many years of a man's life."

"And then, something goes wrong," Barrens said. "I don't know what starts it, or what we can do to stop it." He looked at Steve. "And while I'm reluctant to throw this in your lap so soon after you've gone down there, Steve, that's what I've just about decided to do."

"I'm lost," Steve said. It was now obvious that Barrens was talking about somebody else.

"Didn't Pickens go into this at all with you?" Barrens asked.

"No, sir. I . . . my secretary brought me a copy of the Telex to Mr. Pickens, and I took the first plane I could make."

"Let me coin a phrase for you, Steve," Barrens said. "Haste sometimes makes waste."

"The fact of the matter is, Steve, that we've uncovered a rather nasty mess with your man Chennowith," Tornell said.

"I don't know what you mean."

"Well, I'll spell it out for you," Barrens said. "Frankly, we expected there would be some resistance to our sending you down there, especially after Pickens had recommended Chennowith for the job. But not the amount of resistance, nor the degree of resistance."

"At which point, Haas," Tornell said, "I brought the matter to Mr. Barrens' attention. At the time, it was simply an idea that we should have Mr. Pickens quietly inform Mr. Chennowith that he owed you the same loyalty that he had paid your predecessor. But once we began to look into the matter, rather closely, with the original intent of arranging to transfer Mr. Chennowith elsewhere, we began to uncover all sorts of frankly disturbing information."

"I don't follow this at all," Steve said.

"I don't imagine you've had time to check over the Discretionary Allowance ledger, have you?"

"As a matter of fact, I have. The last two years, anyway. I used some of that money for the company's share of the car, as a matter of fact."

"And you noticed nothing unusual about it?" Barrens asked.

"I noticed that certain funds had been used for travel," Steve said.

"Indeed they have been," Barrens said. "You didn't bring this to Mr. Pickens' attention?"

"No," Steve said. "I didn't."

"To get right to the point, Haas," Barrens said, "after that came to my attention, we did a little looking into things. There have been any number of irregular purchases made at Mr. Chennowith's insistence, which, frankly, don't stand up to scrutiny. The nasty word is kickback."

"I didn't know anything about it," Steve said.

"You could hardly be expected to, in the time you've been there. On the other hand, the decision is yours."

"What decision?" Steve asked.

"Do we ask Mr. Chennowith for his resignation? I don't think we have a legal case which would do us much good, although that possibility is there."

"What are the alternatives?" Steve asked.

"Well, we're not going to permit you to pass him off on someone else in the company, without having

that someone else apprised of the facts. And I rather
doubt, under those conditions, that anyone else
would have him."

"If I read that book correctly, Mr. Barrens, he
shouldn't be in a position to make any decisions I
don't know about."

"That's essentially correct. That rephrases the
question, then, doesn't it? Can you handle him? Or
shall we ask for his resignation?"

"Does he know anything about this yet?"

"Mr. Pickens has told him his future with the company is under discussion."

Steve realized that instead of a feeling of relief that
he wasn't in trouble, he felt even more sick about
this, almost to the point where he would be sick to his
stomach.

"I feel like a sergeant again," Steve said.

"How's that?"

"The way you keep the troops in line is to remove
temptation," he said. "I suppose I can do that here,
too."

"In other words, you're voting to give him another
chance?"

"Yes," Steve said simply. He realized suddenly that
he had known all along that Chennowith was a weak
character; the world was full of people with weak
characters.

"OK," Barrens said. "It's done. He's your responsibility."

"All right," Steve said. He realized he had just accepted a job he didn't want. But keeping a close
watch on Chennowith was better than firing him.

"I think you should know how others felt," Barrens
said. "Mr. Pickens wanted him gone. Mr. Tornell
wanted him gone. I thought he should have another
chance. Perhaps Stu Whitman really was right about
you."

"I beg your pardon?"

"He said that the thing you really had going for you was an ability to think like the boss."

"Oh," Steve said.

"I think you've made a mistake, Haas," Tornell said. "He did a very skillful job—unsuspected by you, apparently—of trying to scuttle your boat. But, in the final analysis, it's your responsibility and your decision."

"If you have any trouble, let me know," Barrens said. "And thank you for coming so quickly. Are you going right back?"

"Yes, I thought I would," Steve said.

"You want to settle this right away, do you?" Barrens asked.

"No," Steve said. "I'm going to let him stew awhile."

"Then what's the rush?"

"I . . . have some personal business to look after," Steve said.

In the company car, on the way back to the airport, Steve thought first about how he would handle Chennowith, and only then about the blonde in the Transportation Department.

Then he wondered if he really was becoming an executive, putting business before pleasure. But that couldn't be. He'd come here expecting to be fired because of the race driving. And they hadn't even mentioned that. He laughed at himself, out loud, and the driver turned around.

"I didn't get that, Mr. Haas?"

"I was just laughing at myself," Steve said.

When the driver was through for the day, he stopped into the dispatcher's office and told him about the weirdo big shot from Atlanta. No eyebrows and he laughed to himself all the way to the airport.

About the Author

W. E. Butterworth was born in New Jersey and educated as a political scientist in Germany, following an 18-month tour in the Army of Occupation in 1946–47. In 1950, he married Emma Macalik, a ballerina of the Vienna State Opera, and shortly after their daughter Patricia (now Mrs. John Hood) was born, he was recalled for service during the Korean War. During his assignment as a combat correspondent with the X Corps in North Korea, he decided to become a writer.

While writing his first novel, he was employed as Information Officer of the Signal Corps Aviation Test & Support Activity at Fort Rucker, Alabama, during the massive build-up of Army Aviation. After his fifteenth book was published, in 1961, he left government employ to write full time. Although his writing encompasses a broad spectrum of adult and young adult fiction and non-fiction, he devotes much of his effort toward automobiles and automobile racing.

Mrs. Butterworth functions as his first editor, working in their home in Fairhope, Alabama. Also at home are their two sons, William E. IV, twelve, and John S. II, seven, Boss and Bandit, twin Llewellyn setters, and Opus, a lovable mutt of unknown ancestry. Among other societies, Mr. Butterworth is a member of the Veterans of Foreign Wars, the American Legion, and the National Association for Stock Car Auto Racing (NASCAR).